VICTORIAN MANSION FLOWER SHOP MYSTERIES

Rooted in Malice

Jan Fields

AnniesFiction.com

Books in the Victorian Mansion Flower Shop Mysteries series

A Fatal Arrangement
Bloomed to Die
The Mistletoe Murder
My Dearly Depotted
Digging Up Secrets
Planted Evidence
Loot of All Evil
Pine and Punishment
Herbal Malady
Deadhead and Buried
The Lily Vanishes
A Cultivated Crime
Suspicious Plots
Weeds of Doubt
Thorn to Secrecy
A Seedy Development
Woes By Any Other Name
Noel Way Out
Rooted in Malice
Absent Without Leaf
Dormant Lies
Best Laid Plants

. . . and more to come!

Rooted in Malice
Copyright © 2019 Annie's.

All rights reserved. No part of this publication may be reproduced, stored in a retrieval system, or transmitted in any form or by any means—electronic, mechanical, photocopying, recording or otherwise—without the prior written permission of the publisher. The only exception is brief quotations in printed reviews. For information address Annie's, 306 East Parr Road, Berne, Indiana 46711-1138.

The characters and events in this book are fictional, and any resemblance to actual persons or events is coincidental.

Library of Congress-in-Publication Data
Rooted in Malice / by Jan Fields
p. cm.
I. Title
                2019934418

AnniesFiction.com
(800) 282-6643
Victorian Mansion Flower Shop Mysteries™
Series Creators: Shari Lohner, Janice Tate
Editor: Elizabeth Morrissey
Cover Illustrator: Bob Kayganich

10 11 12 13 14 | Printed in China | 9 8 7 6 5 4 3 2 1

1

Taking a break from sweeping nonexistent dirt from the hardwood floor, Kaylee Bleu paused near The Flower Patch's tall front window to peer outside at the gray, blustery February afternoon. A lone pickup truck rumbled down Main Street toward Turtle Cove's marina. The lack of traffic—foot or motor—proved more than anything that Washington's Orcas Island was suffering from the winter doldrums, a time when the tourists stayed away and the residents wished for warm spring days. Kaylee for one wasn't looking forward to the next time she had to brave the bone-chilling cold.

As Kaylee resumed her sweeping, her dachshund, Bear, gave a yip from the small, braided rug in front of the cash register counter, as if he'd somehow sensed she had been thinking about how much she didn't want to venture out of the warmth of her flower shop. Kaylee sighed, but offered the little dog a lopsided smile. "I know, buddy. We'll go for a walk as soon as my sweeping is done."

Kaylee's friend and assistant, Mary Bishop, glanced along the shelf of add-on gifts she was dusting. "That'll be the most excitement this place has seen all day," Mary said. "Now that Valentine's Day is over, some of the shops are planning to go to half days or even closing a few days each week until the weather brightens."

"We could try that, I suppose," Kaylee replied absently as she bent over her dustpan. She would prefer to be helping customers, but to be honest, she actually enjoyed sweeping. The swish of the bristles against the floor was both relaxing and purposeful, resulting in neat piles of debris. In a way it reminded her of the peace she found in arranging flowers.

"You sound enthusiastic," Mary said drily as she walked to the next shelf and began carefully dusting each item.

Kaylee shrugged. "I'm not unenthusiastic. Mostly I'm not sure what I'd do with the extra time at home. Much like this place, Wildflower Cottage only requires so much cleaning. I'd catch up on my reading, I suppose. I certainly couldn't get out in my garden."

Mary chuckled. "You're telling me. The only thing growing in my garden this time of year is puddles. Speaking of which, Jess suggested skipping the Petals meeting on Tuesday again."

She referred to their friend Jessica Roberts, a fellow member of the Petal Pushers garden club, which also included another friend, DeeDee Wilcox. They hadn't been meeting regularly due to the weather, and Kaylee was starting to feel downright glum about it—in spite of the fact that all four women worked on the same street, so she still saw her friends nearly every day.

Mary sighed. "I try to remember that all the rain we get now will make Orcas Island burst into bloom in spring."

"That's a good attitude." Kaylee dumped the small amount of dirt she'd swept up into the garbage behind the front counter. "I suppose I could use the extra time to plan my flower beds and maybe brush up on some of the botanical science journal articles I've been collecting."

"Maybe you should try writing one," Mary suggested. "Or maybe a book. It would keep you busy."

Kaylee gaped at her. "What on earth would I write about?"

"Your work with the Orcas Island Sheriff's Department comes to mind."

Kaylee rolled her eyes. "I doubt that would be interesting to anyone."

"I think using forensic botany to solve crimes—including

murders—would be interesting to plenty of people. Academics and otherwise."

"If you say so." Kaylee leaned on her broom. "As for reducing shop hours, I don't want to be closed tomorrow since we do still get some foot traffic on Saturdays. Let's try closing on Monday next week."

Mary's eyebrows shot up, her face the picture of surprise. "I thought talking you into that would be harder. You're actually taking an extra day off?"

Kaylee smiled sheepishly. "Mostly I was giving you another day off. I figured I'd come in and do some bookkeeping and paperwork, though I'll keep the shop closed."

Before Mary could scold Kaylee for being a workaholic—again—the door to the shop opened and Reese Holt walked in. Rain dripped from the brim of the handsome handyman's beloved L.A. Dodgers baseball cap. A partially buttoned heavy coat covered his trademark flannel shirt. Kaylee couldn't help but notice how the coat accentuated Reese's broad shoulders.

"Shopping for flowers?" Kaylee asked. Reese occasionally bought small arrangements for some of his elderly customers to brighten their day—one of the many things Kaylee found endearing about him.

Before Reese could answer, Bear drew his attention by dancing around his feet. Reese laughed and bent to pet the little dog. "I'm glad to see you too, Bear."

Mary dropped her dustcloth on the counter. "I think Bear's lonely. He loves all the attention he gets from customers during the busy months."

"Spring is coming," Reese promised Bear before straightening to give Kaylee a smile that made her heart flutter. "No flower buying today, I'm afraid. I'm just spreading the word that I'll be gone for the next few days, possibly through Wednesday."

Mary came around the counter, her face concerned. "Nothing wrong I hope. No family problems?"

He shook his head. "Everyone's great, though my nephew had a small tree climbing accident and sprained his wrist. Apparently he's trying to claim it as an excuse to eat ice cream for dinner."

Mary laughed. "Sounds like something my Herb would have tried when he was a boy."

Reese grinned. "It's something I might have tried too. I suspect my sister isn't going to fall for it any more than my mom would have, though."

"So what is taking you off the island?" Kaylee asked, a little disappointed at the thought of not seeing Reese for the next few days. *Because we're friends,* she told herself pointedly. *With the island so quiet, I appreciate every moment I spend with my friends.*

Reese's answer pulled her out of her thoughts. "I'm giving a lecture on winter boating safety to a private sailing club in Seattle."

"Sounds fancy," Kaylee said.

"Sounds awful," Reese replied glumly. "I'm happy to help people be safer on the water, but I suspect this talk is mostly their idea of filler entertainment at a club meeting."

"Then why go?" Mary asked.

"One of the club members owns property outside Turtle Cove. I do some work for him during the off-season and handle all the handyman needs for the place. He's a good customer and a good guy, so I didn't want to say no to him. But I would rather not go, especially since the ferry crossing is going to be unpleasant in this rough weather."

"It is awfully windy," Kaylee said, sneaking another glance out the window.

"I'm planning to pack a lunch, but I doubt I'll eat it with how much extra motion there will be." He grinned at Kaylee.

"Speaking of eating, I also wanted to say that I heard last week about a new steak house opening in Eastsound in the spring. They're planning to have outdoor service like O'Brien's. Maybe you'll want to take Bear and try it out when they open."

"O'Brien's has always treated Bear so well," Kaylee said. "It could be risky trying to take him to a new place where they might not welcome him."

Reese's grin wilted. "Good point."

Kaylee was surprised at how disappointed Reese seemed by her reply. She wondered if he knew the owners of the restaurant. *Maybe I should have been more supportive of a new business?*

Before she could ask about his reaction, he said, "I ought to run if I'm going to catch the ferry. I'll see you both when I get back." Bear yipped at his feet and Reese chuckled. "Right, buddy. I'll see all three of you when I get back."

Once Reese had left, Mary arched an eyebrow at Kaylee. "You're going to break his heart."

"What are you talking about?" Kaylee asked.

"He was clearly hinting about a date at that new restaurant," Mary said. "And you shot him right down."

"Oh don't be silly," Kaylee said, though she'd also caught that air of disappointment from him. She and Reese were friends. Sure, they were close friends, and she did find him extremely handsome and kind, and Bear adored him . . . Kaylee gave herself a mental shake. Mary was not going to get her caught up in her matchmaking. "Maybe he thought I'd enjoy hearing about more potentially pet-friendly places."

"Sure," Mary said with a sly grin.

Desperate to head off the rest of this discussion, Kaylee grabbed her coat from the hook and slipped it on. "I'm going next door to get some hot chocolate. I think we need a pick-me-up to get through the afternoon."

"That might be a good idea," Mary said. "A nap is calling me, but cocoa sounds better."

Bear hadn't missed Kaylee shrugging into her jacket, and he raced to the shop door and danced around with his tail wagging furiously. Kaylee bent to pat him on the head. "Sorry, Bear. No dogs at the bakery. You stay here with Mary, and I promise we'll have a nice walk soon."

Bear clearly realized the message in her tone because his enthusiasm subsided immediately. Even his jaunty red bow tie seemed to droop.

"You are not making me feel guilty," Kaylee lied. "We had that nice walk before I started cleaning. You're not fooling me."

Bear licked her hand once, then returned to moping. Mary walked over and swept him up in her arms. "I'll comfort him in his despair while you're gone."

Kaylee chuckled. "Thanks. Don't stuff him with treats."

As soon as Kaylee pulled the door open, the wind blasted her, whipping up her long, dark hair and making her eyes sting. She pulled the knit hat from the pocket of her jacket and tugged it on with the hope of avoiding a tangled mess from the wind playing hairdresser.

The trek to Death by Chocolate was short since the bakery was right next door, but Kaylee was still glad to get out of the cold. The wind had picked up since the walk she'd taken with Bear earlier and she hoped it would blow itself out soon. When she pulled on the door to the bakery, a gust tried to jerk it out of her hands, and it took real effort to pull the door closed again.

"Kaylee Bleu! I didn't think you had the grit to get out in this kind of wind."

Kaylee pushed the hair out of her eyes and faced Roz Corzo. The tall, burly woman owned a boat down at the marina and used it to guide whale watches and fishing tours for tourists. One look at Roz would convince anyone that she wasn't the sort to be intimidated by wind or much of anything else. Her hair was mostly gray and cut short, and her skin was aged beyond her years from all the time spent outdoors. She wore a heavy fisherman's sweater with baggy jeans tucked into worn boots.

"Nice to see you, Roz," Kaylee said.

Roz barked out a laugh and elbowed the woman beside her. "She's lying, of course."

"Don't be that way," the other woman said. Like Roz, this woman was tall, but she lacked Roz's muscles and broad shoulders. Instead, her frame was willowy and her dark hair hung down her back in a tidy French braid. She wore a floral silk scarf around her neck and a stylish wool coat. "I'm Jeanette Colson." The woman offered Kaylee her hand. "I used to live on the island years ago."

"Oh, maybe you knew my grandparents," Kaylee suggested. "Ed and Bea Lyons?"

Jeanette's expression lit up in recollection. "I certainly did. They were always incredibly nice to me, and I'll be the first to admit, I wasn't always the easiest person to be nice to."

"That's all right," Roz growled. "They were even nice to me. It was spooky."

That made Kaylee laugh. Roz could be abrasive, but it was hard to outright dislike anyone so aware of her own shortcomings. "We all have our moments."

Roz narrowed her eyes at Kaylee. "Really? I ain't seen yours yet, Miss Perfect."

"Stop," Jeanette said airily, waving her hand at Roz before focusing on Kaylee. "I think she acts that way to see if she can provoke everyone into being as grumpy as she is. Now, if you're living on the island, you must be helping Bea and Mary with the flower shop?"

"Bea retired and moved to Arizona," Kaylee said. "But I run the shop with Mary. She's there now."

The cheerful expression darkened a bit, but Jeanette kept a smile on her face. "I'll have to run by and say hello if I have a chance before I leave."

For whatever reason, Kaylee suspected Jeanette wasn't being honest. Did she have some problem with Mary? Kaylee pushed down the idea. "Are you staying long?"

"Only through the weekend," Jeanette answered. "I have to head to work early next week, but I wanted to spend some time with Roz. Sometimes it's good to be with someone who's in on all your secrets, especially the ones about your ex. Isn't that right, Roz?"

Roz scowled at her. "Richard wasn't my ex, Jeanette. He died."

Jeanette winced. "Of course. Sorry. I was talking about Bart." She dropped her voice to a conspiratorial whisper, leaning toward Kaylee. "That's probably why I have an ex. I'm too self-absorbed." She gestured toward the counter where Jessica Roberts, the bakery owner, held up a white box. "I believe our goodies are ready."

"No hurry," Jessica said. "I didn't want to interrupt your conversation."

Roz huffed. "If you don't interrupt Jeanette, you'll never get to talk."

"It's true," Jeanette said as she collected the box and handed money to Jessica. "We ought to share these with your neighbor. It might soften the old grouch up."

"I'm not wasting any treats on Pop Ronson," Roz retorted. "That man is a menace."

"He'd be fine if you didn't go out of your way to antagonize him," Jeanette said. "He's nice enough to me, if a little cranky."

Thankfully, once we get the boat out, you two will be too far apart to fight."

"You're still on about taking the boat out tonight?" Roz huffed. "That doesn't make a lick of sense with this wind. And I've barely had any sleep since you arrived. Can't we have dinner at the inn and hit the sack early? We could take the boat out first thing tomorrow."

Kaylee glanced toward the windows where she could see the wind whipping branches on the shrubs in the planter boxes across the street. It was obviously a terrible night to be on the water. Kaylee had a strong stomach, but she suspected that would put it to the test. Taking a boat out on the ocean in these conditions might even be dangerous.

"Don't be such an old lady," Jeanette said. "I love being at sea in the winter here. It's more of a contest, a battle with the elements."

"One that not every boat wins," Jessica warned. "This kind of weather is treacherous, especially at night."

Roz glared at Jessica. "I know the waters here far better than you do. And I know my boat." She whipped her head toward Jeanette. "Let's go. If we're going out in this weather, I've got things to check."

Roz stomped out the door, letting in a blast of cold air in the process. Jeanette eyed Kaylee and Jessica then shrugged before following her friend. "Don't worry. I'll bring a life raft along."

"Oh dear." Jessica put both hands to her pixie-like face after the door closed. "I think I said exactly the wrong thing. Now Roz is sure to go out, if only to be contrary."

Kaylee had to admit that might be a possibility. "She does have a lot of experience though. And it's still hours before dark. Maybe with some time to think about it, both of them will change their minds."

"I hope so," Jessica said, then cocked her head at Kaylee.

"Did you come in for something?"

Kaylee laughed. "Right. Sorry. Can I have two hot chocolates, please? Mary and I could use a boost from our rather slow morning."

"I understand that," Jessica said as she set about preparing the hot chocolate. She warmed cream, shaved chocolate, and pure cocoa—no packaged powder for Death by Chocolate customers. "Roz and her friend actually qualified as a rush of customers today."

"Honestly, it's a bit surprising to me that Roz has an old friend who is as outgoing as Jeanette," Kaylee said. "Jeanette must be truly committed to the friendship to come and visit in February, though I suppose it's every bit as gray and rainy in Seattle. I haven't forgotten the winter doldrums from my years at the university."

"We don't get quite as much rain as Seattle," Jessica agreed. "Though I think we get more wind. A boat ride certainly would be lively. Even the fishing boats don't go out in this kind of wind. Jeanette must *love* boats to even suggest it."

Kaylee wrinkled her nose. "I enjoy boats, but I'm not a fan of seasickness." Then a thought hit her. "Who's that Pop guy they were talking about?"

"Pop Ronson? He runs whale watches and fishing trips from the marina, the same as Roz. His boat, *The Misty Maid*, is in the slip right next to Roz's. The two are constantly yelling at one another from the decks of their boats. Nick has been called out more than once for noise complaints."

Surprised that their friend Deputy Nick Durham had responded to such a call, Kaylee asked, "Roz can yell that loud?"

"Apparently they bought bullhorns at one point," Jessica said as she stirred the cups of hot chocolate vigorously. "Nick confiscated at least one of those, as I remember."

Kaylee pictured two grizzled boat captains blasting derisive comments at each other. The image made her giggle. "Any idea what caused the feud between the two of them?"

"He and Roz have been at it for years. Pop can't understand how Roz gets more business than he does considering she's a . . . challenging personality. He's always coming up with theories about how she's cheating him." Jessica chuckled. "You should hear some of the conspiracy theories he's come up with. One of them involved Roz using some kind of illegal technology, stolen from the government, that makes the whales show up more for her boat than for his."

Since Kaylee knew full well that Jessica was fond of conspiracy theories of all sorts, she was surprised that her friend would laugh at someone else's outlandish theories. "What do you think it is?"

Jessica lifted one shoulder in a small shrug, then topped each cup of hot chocolate with a generous dollop of whipped cream. "Honestly, I can't imagine. It's a mystery." She snapped the lids on the cups.

"One I believe I'll ignore," Kaylee said as she handed over money. "I have more cleaning to do at the shop. Thanks for the chat, and for the chocolate of course."

Jessica pushed the two cups of hot chocolate into a small cardboard carrier to make it easier for Kaylee to hold both cups with one hand. As Kaylee picked them up, her eye was drawn to the lavender geranium that Jessica kept on the end of the counter. Jessica treated the plant like a pet, down to naming it Oliver. According to Jessica, Oliver was unusually sensitive to danger and hostility around him, and the plant drooped to warn Jessica of impending doom.

As always, Oliver was healthy and bright. Though Jessica fussed over the plant, she clearly didn't give in to an urge to overwater him or any of the other habits people sometimes fell into when they loved a potted plant a bit too much. Still, as

Kaylee examined the healthy little plant, a frilly green leaf fell off onto the counter.

"Did you see that?" Jessica squeaked in horror.

Kaylee picked up the leaf. It showed no signs of wilt and lacked the dark edges she'd expect from a leaf about to fall. She pointed toward the door. "It was probably weakened by all the wind coming in."

"And decided to fall right now?" Disbelief was clear in Jessica's tone. "Nope, Oliver can tell something is wrong. I'm sure of it." She peered directly into Kaylee's eyes. "And remember, he dropped a leaf as you were looking at him. I think the warning is for you."

Kaylee forced a smile. "Don't worry, Oliver. I'm fine."

"Don't take this too lightly, Kaylee. I mean it. Be careful for the next day or so, okay?"

"I'll be careful," Kaylee promised. She headed out into the wind, but it wasn't only the weather that sent a cold chill through her. As much as she didn't want to give any credence to a warning made by a plant, Kaylee couldn't shake off the creepy sensation tickling her spine.

2

"I was beginning to worry that you'd gotten blown away," Mary said with a laugh when Kaylee entered The Flower Patch, the wind giving her an extra shove through the doorway.

"Sorry about that." Kaylee pulled one of the cups from the holder and handed it to Mary before bending to pat Bear as he danced around her feet. "I ran into Roz Corzo and a friend of hers, a woman named Jeanette Colson. She mentioned your name."

Mary frowned slightly. "I remember Jeanette. She's been gone a long time. What brings her to Turtle Cove?"

"Visiting Roz, apparently." Kaylee shrugged out of her jacket and hung it up. "I take it by the frown that Jeanette wasn't one of your favorite people."

Mary took a long sip of her hot chocolate, which Kaylee suspected was a stalling gesture. "I didn't know her all that well, but she was a bit too fond of drama, I thought," Mary said finally. "Divorce is ugly enough without letting it become a circus. And I always thought she seemed especially focused on getting sympathy from your grandparents." She shook her head. "I'll be honest—I didn't miss her when she left."

Kaylee thought about that a bit as she sipped her own hot chocolate. Even distracted by her thoughts, she was aware of the creamy, rich liquid restoring the warmth that the biting wind had sucked away. When she felt thawed, she said, "Jessica didn't remember Jeanette."

"I'm not surprised," Mary said. "The only reason I knew her was because of Bea and Ed. Jeanette was never community-minded, but she latched on to your grandparents fiercely. She used to come into the shop to pour out some new tale of her husband's transgressions. Bea is kind, understanding, and often sympathetic, but at some point she'd always try to get Jeanette to see Bart's side, and that's when the woman would stomp out in a huff. She was never terribly interested in other people's viewpoints."

"She and Roz make an unlikely pair," Kaylee said. "Roz doesn't seem the type to let other people take advantage of her much."

"You might be surprised," Mary said. "Roz isn't exactly social, but everyone needs a friend. Even if it's a toxic one."

Kaylee raised her eyebrows. "Jeanette was *that* bad?"

Mary sighed and waved off the question. "Don't mind me. It's been years and the woman annoyed me to no end, so I may be remembering her unfairly. Though in my defense, I will add that Ed eventually put a stop to her coming out to the house. He said Jeanette always upset Bea. Jeanette left the island right after that."

Before Mary could comment again, the shop door opened and a young couple came in, laughing as they struggled to close the door.

"We made it," the young man said. "Now how do we buy flowers and get them home without being blown away?"

Kaylee smiled brightly, happy to have customers at last. "I'm sure we can figure something out. Are you looking for anything specific?"

The wind seemed to blow itself out by Monday morning, and Kaylee was almost sorry she'd decided not to open the shop. The weather wasn't exactly welcoming, but it did seem brighter. Kaylee could almost believe spring really was coming in a matter of weeks. In honor of that idea, she chose a bow tie for Bear that featured tiny daisies sprinkled all over the green fabric.

Kaylee locked the shop door behind her and headed up to her second-floor office with Bear scampering up the steps beside her. When they reached the office, Bear immediately ran over to stare pointedly at the filing cabinet where Kaylee kept a bag of treats for him.

"No treats yet," she said with mild reproof. "You just had breakfast. You're going to become a little brown watermelon if I give you as many treats as you want."

Bear offered a yip of disagreement, but he gave up and trotted to his dog bed to chew on a squeaky dog toy. Kaylee settled behind the weathered desk and was soon completely wrapped up in numbers and paperwork, with only the quiet squeaks as background music.

When pounding erupted on the door downstairs, both Kaylee and Bear jumped. Bear launched into a flurry of barking and raced for the stairs, clearly intent on defending the shop.

"Hush, Bear," Kaylee called as she followed him. "I get it. Someone is at the door."

Bear subsided into low growls, and Kaylee figured that was the best she was going to get until the person at the door stopped pounding. When she reached the bottom of the stairs and could see through the front door, Kaylee felt a fresh burst of surprise. Roz stood out on the porch, glaring into the shop with her signature scowl. She wore a knit cap over her gray curls and held her arms stiffly by her side, her hands in tight fists.

Watching the furious woman, Kaylee had a fleeting thought that it might be better to leave the door between them. Then she pushed that down. She *knew* Roz. She wasn't scared of her.

"We'd best find out what's going on," she murmured to Bear, then flipped the lock and pulled the door open.

Roz stomped in, virtually pushing Kaylee aside. "You have to help me!"

"Help you with what?" Kaylee glanced up and down the porch before closing the door, in case Roz's friend Jeanette was waiting outside. No one should have to wait in the cold. There was no sign of Jeanette, so she closed and locked the door, then turned to face Roz.

"Jeanette is missing," Roz announced, her hands on her hips. "And the cops think I killed her."

"Hold on. Let's go to the kitchen and sit down with some coffee to talk about this. Okay?"

Years before, her grandmother had impressed upon Kaylee the magic of a warm drink. "It's hard to fight over a cup of tea or a good mug of coffee," Bea had said. "A warm beverage is like getting a hug in a cup. Never underestimate its value when someone is upset."

Kaylee was glad to see Bea was correct, as always, when Roz huffed and relaxed the tiniest bit, shoving her still fisted hands into the deep pockets of her heavy coat. "Yeah, coffee would be good."

Once they were seated at the small table and chairs in the kitchen with steaming mugs, Kaylee brought the conversation back to Roz's opening remark. "Why would the police possibly believe you killed anyone?"

Roz set her mug down on the table with enough force that the coffee sloshed nearly over the side. "Well, you remember how Jeanette wanted to take the boat out on Friday night?"

Kaylee nodded.

"I tried to talk her out of it," Roz said. "I'm no coward, but I was tired, and the water was unusually rough. I try to take care of my boat. It's the only livelihood I've got." Roz paused and stared into her coffee mug.

"It certainly didn't seem a fit night for boating," Kaylee prompted.

"Jeanette wouldn't let up. She's always been that way. She even offered to bring along a life raft," Roz grumbled. "You should have seen her schlepping this huge duffel and claiming I was a wimp when I tried to back out after we left Death by Chocolate."

"But you finally agreed," Kaylee said.

"Yeah, I finally agreed, and we took the boat out after we picked up some dinner to go at O'Brien's. I sure wasn't going to try to cook on the boat in that weather."

Roz stalled again, making Kaylee wonder why. Usually when Roz had a full head of steam, coaxing wasn't necessary. Kaylee sat quietly, sipping her own coffee and waiting for Roz to continue, which she eventually did.

"After we ate, I broke out the pastries from the bakery. Jeanette insisted on making us some tea to go with them." Roz wrinkled her nose in disgust. "I don't usually drink tea. Water that you wash dried weeds in doesn't strike me as a beverage."

Kaylee didn't bother arguing with that, though she enjoyed a good cup of tea. "Why do you have tea on board if you don't care for it? For clients?"

Roz reared back, as if the very idea of stocking something for clients was offensive. "Hardly," she scoffed. "If clients want something, they best pack a picnic. No, Jeanette brought the tea with her. She said she made it herself with rubbish right from her own garden."

Kaylee raised an eyebrow, rather doubting Jeanette had called her plants *rubbish*.

Roz saw the expression and misinterpreted it. "You should have heard her. She talked it up like it was the elixir of the gods or something, claiming health benefits like a television huckster. I drank it to shut her up. And I can tell you, it was noxious. Weed water, it was, and bitter to boot."

Kaylee was beginning to wonder if Roz was ever going to get to the point or if she was simply going to continue harping on about her hatred of tea. But then Roz slapped a hand down on the table, making Kaylee jump and eliciting an annoyed growl from Bear on the floor by Kaylee's feet.

"Right after I finished the vile stuff, I started getting sleepy. I could hardly hold my head up. I was tired, but this wasn't natural, I tell you. I guess I passed out."

Kaylee sat up straighter. The story was getting interesting after all. "Do you think Jeanette put something in the tea?"

"I'd hate to think that, but I haven't come up with anything else," Roz said. "I didn't wake up until Saturday morning. My boat was adrift, and Jeanette was missing. So was that stupid duffel with the life raft in it."

"So you believe she used the raft to get off your boat? Would an inflatable raft be safe in that weather?"

"Of course not," Roz snapped. "My own boat was barely safe in that weather." She dropped her gaze to her coffee again, and the vitality drained from her voice as she continued her story. "I called the Coast Guard. All day Saturday and Sunday I searched the area where we'd been when I was last awake. I also called her phone, in case she'd gotten off the boat in some normal way, but nothing. I have no idea what happened to Jeanette."

"What if she was unaware the tea was tainted somehow?" Kaylee suggested. "Maybe she got tired too, and staggered to the deck and fell over."

"I thought that at first, but why would she have taken the duffel?" Roz's expression was stricken. "I shouldn't have gone out. We should have stayed on shore. I knew it was a bad idea." She rubbed her hand over her face.

Kaylee frowned. "You said the police believe you killed Jeanette. What would make you think that?"

"Jeanette's ex-husband, Bart, insists I must have killed her and dumped her body overboard. He called the sheriff's department and demanded they arrest me. They didn't, of course, but they did poke around my boat as if they thought I might be a smuggler." Roz spat out the word *smuggler*.

"Did they find anything?" Kaylee asked.

Roz's gaze snapped to Kaylee's. "I didn't do anything."

"Did they find anything?" Kaylee repeated, gently but firmly.

"Blood." Roz slumped, cradling her head in her hands. "It's no big deal. I sometimes take fishermen out. Of course there's going to be blood. Deep-sea fishing makes a mess." She raised her head again. "I work hard to keep my boat clean, but blood is hard to get out. I'm sure they found nothing but fish blood, but in the meanwhile, I'm not allowed to take my boat out. How am I supposed to make a living?"

"Did you have any charters lined up?" Kaylee asked.

"Well, no," Roz answered grudgingly. "People don't exactly flock to the island this time of year. But the sheriff's department doesn't even care. I *might* have had clients."

Kaylee ignored Roz's wounded tone. "Why would Jeanette's ex-husband accuse you of murder?"

"Because he's a skunk." Roz spun her empty mug in slow circles in her hands. "Jeanette hated the guy's guts by the time they divorced, and the feeling was mutual." She narrowed her eyes. "If anyone was going to murder Jeanette, it would have been Bart. Mark my words."

"Did you say that to the sheriff?" Kaylee asked.

Roz harrumphed. "As if they cared about *my* opinion."

"If someone killed Jeanette, and it wasn't an accident, the killer would probably have been on the island. Was Bart here?"

Roz shrugged heavily. "He could have been. He has a boat. He might even have Jeanette right now. Maybe he came out to my boat and kidnapped her. Maybe he found some way to slip something into Jeanette's tea stash and then followed us out in the boat. As soon as I passed out, he grabbed her." She tapped her forefinger on the table for emphasis. "Jeanette told me that he never did get over her. She said he'd called, begging her to come back to him. After all these years, you'd think that man would have some pride."

Kaylee could see how the sheriff's department could be less than impressed with Roz's theories, since Roz couldn't seem to keep them straight herself. *Is Jeanette's ex-husband obsessed with her or does he hate her?* Still, as far as Kaylee was concerned, there was a bigger question. "So, how does this concern me?"

Roz pointed at her. "I know how nosy you are. And how you've figured out all kinds of stuff that the sheriff's department couldn't sort out. Now, I need you to put your nosy ways to good use. Find Jeanette and prove I didn't have anything to do with her disappearance. This morning, three different people asked me if I was still drunk." Her face darkened further.

"Why would anyone think you were drunk?"

"That's the gossip network theory about all this. Folks are saying I was so drunk that I had some kind of blackout, but I don't even drink. I'm telling you, all I had was tea. One disgusting cup of tea!" Roz's voice rose enough to elicit a warning growl from Bear.

Kaylee gave him a calming rub on the head, then reached out and patted Roz's arm. She wasn't exactly enthusiastic about being called nosy, but she had to agree that Roz was in a bind. "I can't guarantee I'll find anything useful, but I can ask a few questions."

Roz nodded her head slowly. "And if you hear anyone repeating that drunk rumor, you tell them Roz Corzo doesn't drink, you hear?"

"I will," Kaylee said. "But I can't promise that anything I do or say will make much difference."

"That's okay." Roz stood slowly and handed Kaylee her empty mug. "I never trust people who promise too much. You're a good sort. Kind of a princess, but all right. Your grandparents were too."

Kaylee rose to her feet and set the mugs in the sink, trying to sort out if Roz had been complimenting her or insulting her. As she escorted Roz to the front door, Kaylee could see the boat captain slumping as if telling her story had drained her of much of the energy she'd brought into the shop. "You should try to get some rest," Kaylee said as she unlocked the door.

Roz nodded without saying anything and headed out into the chilly morning.

Kaylee closed and locked the door behind Roz, then her gaze fell on Bear's eager face. "So, what did happen to Jeanette Colson?" Bear yipped, and Kaylee nodded. "You're right. We should find out. And I have a good idea of where to start."

3

After Roz left, Kaylee tried to focus on her paperwork, wanting to finish it up before making the phone calls that would start her investigation. Try as she might, though, Roz's problem wouldn't let her concentrate. At heart, she trusted the Orcas Island Sheriff's Department to get to the bottom of Jeanette's disappearance. Kaylee knew the department was full of competent, committed people, but she simply couldn't stop the swirl of questions in her head. After the third time she lost track of the numbers she was trying to add, she sighed so deeply that Bear whined and stood up against her knee with concern in his brown eyes.

"It's okay, Bear," Kaylee said as she bent to rub his ears. "I just can't get Roz's friend out of my head. I think I ought to ask Nick about it. Once I talk to him, I'll probably be able to get to work." She smiled at Bear. "How would you like a walk to see your favorite deputy?"

Bear began dancing around, wagging his tail fiercely. Kaylee stood and stretched before heading downstairs to grab Bear's leash from the hook behind the front counter. When they stepped outside, Kaylee realized that the day's ample sunshine and lack of wind were deceptive. She couldn't help but shiver as the frigid air sucked all the warmth from her face. "The temperature is dropping," she told Bear. "Let's go grab your coat from the car. I don't want you getting a chill."

Kaylee led her dog down the sidewalk toward the spot where she'd left her red Ford Escape. She normally parked behind the flower shop, but with so little street traffic, she had parked on the street in the hopes that a sunny parking space would result in a marginally warmer car. She'd barely gotten halfway there when she heard a familiar voice call her name. Bear yipped excitedly, and Kaylee put her hand across her forehead to block the sun as she glanced across the street toward the source of the voice. Just as she'd thought, it was Deputy Nick Durham.

"You are exactly the man I need to see," Kaylee called out.

Nick glanced both ways then crossed Main Street, his eyebrow raised in question. "Are you having some trouble?" he asked as he reached Kaylee and Bear.

"Not me," Kaylee said. "But I do have something I want to talk with you about. Can you spare a few minutes?"

"Sure. I was about to run into Death by Chocolate for some coffee and a chance to thaw out. You can join me if you want."

Kaylee waved toward Bear. "I can't bring him in. But if you'll take him back to the flower shop for me, I'll buy two coffees to go. I promise my shop is warm as toast."

"It's a deal," Nick said, then accepted the leash and keys from Kaylee. "Come on, Bear. Let's get out of the cold."

Bear followed his friend agreeably, which confirmed Kaylee's suspicion that the little dog was too cold. Bear rarely accepted having a walk shortened—not graciously anyway.

She grabbed Bear's small jacket from her car so she'd be ready for a walk later, then hurried to Death by Chocolate. The bakery had no line at the register, but a handful of warmly dressed patrons sat sipping coffee and chatting at small tables.

Jessica's face lit up when she saw Kaylee. "I didn't think I'd see you today since you aren't open. Coffee?"

"Two, please," Kaylee said. "I came in to catch up on paperwork."

Jessica poured the coffee. "You and Mary?"

Kaylee shook her head. "Nick is waiting for me at the shop though. I had something I wanted to talk with him about."

Jessica's almond-shaped eyes widened, and she leaned closer to Kaylee, lowering her voice to avoid being overheard by the other customers. "You mean the murder?"

Kaylee frowned. "We're not sure anyone died."

"Oliver is sure," Jessica murmured. "He dropped another leaf Friday night. I found it on Saturday morning when I came in. Two leaves in one day! I knew something horrible must have happened." Shaking her head slowly, she secured lids on the two paper cups of coffee, then set them on the counter in front of Kaylee. "You tell me what you find out, okay?"

"I will." Kaylee counted out her money. "Unless I'm sworn to secrecy."

When she got to The Flower Patch, Kaylee found Nick perched on the edge of the love seat in her consultation area, rubbing Bear's belly as he lay in utter bliss on the floor.

"Bear was already your friend for life," Kaylee said as she handed Nick his coffee and settled in one of the comfy slipper chairs. "But the occasional belly rub seals the deal for sure."

Nick laughed before taking a sip of his coffee. "I have to stay on Bear's good side. He's come through for me on more than one investigation. And I think I'm going to need all the help I can get this time."

Kaylee leaped on the opening. "And speaking of investigations and help—"

Nick groaned and held up a hand. "All right, I walked into that one, but I can't give out details of an ongoing investigation. Don't try that innocent act on me. This is not our first rodeo."

"Fine," Kaylee said. "But Roz was here this morning in a panic. She's sure she's about to be railroaded for the death of her friend. I was hoping to hear something to calm her nerves."

"I didn't know you and Roz were pals. I didn't know Roz and *anyone* were pals, honestly."

"I rather doubt Roz would use the word *pals*," Kaylee said. "Especially not when she called me nosy. But she's scared and she practically demanded I do something. Chatting with you is simple self-defense."

Bear pawed at Nick's shin, so the deputy resumed his petting. "That sounds about right with Roz. Strictly off the record, I can't see Roz as a murderer unless you can grumble someone to death. And we have no particular reason to believe Roz did anything wrong. She definitely did something stupid, taking that boat out on Friday night in that weather. However, if the sheriff's department started arresting people for being boneheaded, the jail would fill up pretty fast."

"Roz said Jeanette's ex is calling her a killer."

Nick relaxed and took a long sip of his coffee. "Our investigations are not directed by the rantings of people in grief."

"Roz also asked me to do what I could to counter the rumor that she'd been drinking," Kaylee said.

Nick's face took on a faintly amused expression. "I'd heard that one. Roz voluntarily submitted to a blood test on Saturday morning. It came back negative for alcohol or drugs."

Kaylee sat up straighter at that news. "Roz seemed to think she might have been drugged by the tea she drank."

"If she was, it was nothing a normal toxicology screen could pick up." Nick peered at Kaylee shrewdly. "But we do have the dregs from the tea. Do you think you could examine it for me and tell me what plants were involved and whether anything was in there that shouldn't have been?"

"I would be happy to," Kaylee said. "But remember, my skill set is plants. You're going to need to retain some of the dregs for a more thorough chemical analysis."

"I'll take any help you can give." Nick sat back, holding his cup between both hands. Bear gave him reproving glances before giving up and relocating a few feet to sit by Kaylee's chair. "I can bring the samples by late tomorrow morning if that works for you."

"It should be fine," Kaylee said. "And in exchange, can you tell me what you thought of Jeanette's ex? Roz said the man owns a boat. What if his insistence that Roz killed Jeanette is a smoke screen for his own guilt?"

Nick shrugged. "Sounds a bit convoluted. He's supposed to be coming in on the next ferry and it's my job to meet him, which is why I didn't ask you to do the analysis today. Based on our phone conversation, I'm not excited about interviewing this guy. Grief is unpredictable and makes people say and do things they wouldn't otherwise."

"Well," Kaylee said slyly, "I still owe Bear the rest of his walk. How about we go with you to the port? Bear loves meeting the ferry."

"You're not planning to stay out of this, are you?" Nick asked.

"If I'm not mistaken, you just asked me to get involved by analyzing the tea," Kaylee pointed out. "But I certainly don't intend to get in your way."

"I should scold you," Nick said, "but I don't mind the moral support. And you might be better at calming the irate ex than I am." He chugged down the rest of his coffee and stood. "Ready to go?"

"Just let me get Bear ready."

With the added warmth of his jacket, Bear was delighted to be going on a walk, and Kaylee could tell he was especially happy to be joined by his good buddy Nick. While they walked, Nick didn't talk much, and Kaylee assumed he was focused on the uncomfortable meeting to come.

As they headed up the street, she noticed that most of the trendier, tourist-dependent shops were closed. Some had only weekend hours until the end of winter. She tugged her coat closer around her neck, and thought about her years living in Seattle. Orcas Island wasn't so different in February, though she thought it offered more impressive views.

Nick must have noticed her tugging on her jacket. "Are you too cold? You don't have to come along. The dock is going to be even chillier."

"I don't mind," Kaylee said. "I was thinking this isn't so very different from living in Seattle. More peaceful and more beautiful, though."

"You really don't miss university life?"

"I miss some of the people," Kaylee admitted, "but I've made amazing friends here, and I feel connected to the island in ways that are hard to explain."

"Me too. I couldn't imagine leaving Orcas Island."

They reached the marina where the ferry docked, and Kaylee looked down toward the slip where Roz's boat was moored. She saw no sign of the woman herself.

"Is Roz allowed on her boat yet?" Kaylee asked.

"Not yet," Nick said. "We still have some techs processing evidence. It shouldn't be much longer."

"She was worried about it."

He huffed. "Everyone is always worried about being inconvenienced."

Kaylee poked his arm gently. "You're starting to sound like Roz."

"It's been that kind of weekend." He pointed. "There's the ferry."

Kaylee scooped Bear up to keep him warm as they waited for the ferry to dock and the people to file off. In the summer, the ferry would be packed with tourists and cars, but now barely a handful of people stepped off, all huddled in their coats.

One stocky, red-faced man wearing a knit cap and a scowl

paused just off the gangplank and peered around. The man's clothes were bulky and rough, reminding Kaylee of the kind of cold-weather gear she'd seen Roz wear. He spotted Nick's uniform and stormed toward them. The heavy canvas duffel slung over his shoulder didn't slow him down any.

Kaylee took an involuntary step back as the man barreled toward them. She couldn't remember the last time she'd seen anyone so visibly hostile. The man pointed at Nick. "Roz Corzo better be in jail," he bellowed. "Or I'm suing everyone in your department."

Nick didn't flinch at the man's rage. Instead, he spoke in an especially calm, quiet tone. "Mr. Bart Marlow, I assume."

The man's face registered surprise at the question before returning to its previous hostility. "I hope your police work is better than that. I'm Lyle Colson. Jeanette was my sister."

"Sorry, I wasn't aware you were coming over on the early ferry," Nick said evenly. "We still haven't found out what happened to your sister beyond that she's missing. Are you saying you have more information than the Orcas Island Sheriff's Department?"

The man snorted. "I expect almost everyone has more information than your lot. But my sister wouldn't up and disappear at sea. She isn't a bird. She couldn't have flown off the boat."

"Apparently she had an inflatable raft," Kaylee said, getting scowls from both Nick and Jeanette's brother. Kaylee shrugged at Nick. "The duffel with the raft is missing, isn't it?"

Before Nick could say anything, Lyle snapped, "I don't know what you're talking about, lady. That Corzo woman killed my sister. I demand she be arrested."

"I'm not sure that what you want is necessarily going to drive this case," Nick said, irritation edging briefly into his voice then disappearing. "But I can assure you that our investigation will be thorough. We're considering everyone who may have come in contact with Ms. Colson." The deputy looked past Lyle and called out. "Is there a Bart Marlow here?"

The man who came forward wore a better grade of clothing than Jeanette's brother, with a plaid scarf wrapped around his neck above the collar of his long wool jacket. The one similarity to Lyle's outfit was the knit cap on his head. Jeanette's ex-husband carried a neat leather overnight bag in one hand and raised his free hand at Nick's question. "That's me."

Nick waved him over. "You might as well join the circus."

Bart ambled toward them. "I'm not interested in any dramatic announcements about lawsuits. I want to see justice done for my wife. The one thing I do agree with Lyle about is Roz. It's clear that she's a murderer, plain and simple."

"I'm starting to think nothing about this case is going to be simple," Nick muttered, then announced, "The only thing that is clear is that we need to have a long chat. Why are you both so convinced of Mrs. Corzo's guilt?"

"Why aren't you?" Lyle growled. He narrowed his eyes. "I heard that people close ranks on these little islands. Shut out the outsiders, right? Protect your own."

"Nick isn't that way," Kaylee insisted, and both strangers glowered at her. She felt a frisson of alarm, and Bear growled deep in his chest.

The two men might have different approaches, but Kaylee felt they had one thing in common. In one way or another, both of them could be dangerous. Very dangerous.

4

Resisting the urge to shy away from the intensity of the two men staring at her, Kaylee raised her chin slightly and said, "I only met Jeanette briefly, but she was a friend of my grandparents. You both must be so worried over her whereabouts."

"Are you with the police?" Lyle demanded.

"Miss Bleu is a civilian consultant," Nick said. "She helps us out now and then, when her specialty is of use."

Lyle kept his gaze on Kaylee, inspecting her as if she were an interesting bug he might be considering squashing. "And what specialty is that?"

"Forensic botany," Kaylee replied, channeling all the professorial dignity she'd learned from her years on the faculty at the University of Washington. The man's antagonism was certainly intimidating, but she absolutely refused to give in to the tactics of a bully. "I identify plants."

"And you find a lot of plants on boats in the middle of the ocean?" Bart asked. His tone was mild, but his attention was no less focused than Lyle's.

"Hold on, gentlemen," Nick interrupted, and Kaylee resisted the urge to sigh in relief when the deputy succeeded in drawing the men's attention. "We're getting way off track here, and I am definitely not enjoying standing out in the cold. Why don't we go somewhere more comfortable?"

"And where exactly do you propose we go?" Lyle sneered.

Beyond the men's heads, Kaylee noticed a tall woman in a long, dark coat trimmed in faux fur casting curious glances at them. The coat was unbuttoned in the front, showing off a business suit, which made Kaylee wonder how the woman wasn't freezing. For an instant, Kaylee locked eyes with the woman, but the stranger dropped her gaze almost immediately and hurried past them with her head lowered.

"Mr. Marlow," Nick said. "You told me on the phone that you'd be staying at the Northern Lights Inn. They have a very nice dining room that serves coffee and pastries all day. Why don't we move the discussion there, where it's warmer?"

"A little cold doesn't bother me any," Lyle said. "I've been in worse."

His former brother-in-law huffed a mirthless laugh. "I don't think it's a contest. Moving our conversation to the inn sounds good to me. Where are you staying, Lyle?"

"I don't have a room yet." Lyle's expression stayed mulish, but Kaylee saw him shiver when a chill hit them from off the water. "I suppose I could see if they have any rooms available at that inn."

"Then it would be in our best interest to take this conversation there." Nick pointed toward some dark clouds that were already casting deep shadows over the water as they moved toward Turtle Cove. "If we spend much longer out here, we're definitely going to get wet."

"I'd prefer to avoid that," Bart said.

"It'd be a shame for Bart to muss his nice clothes," Lyle said, scorn dripping from every word. "We can go on to the inn."

"You coming?" Bart asked Kaylee, his head to one side. "Did you say you knew Jeanette?"

"I met her briefly Friday afternoon at the bakery next to my shop." She held out her hand, holding Bear close to her chest with the other. "I'm Kaylee Bleu. My grandparents are Ed and Bea Lyons."

Kaylee couldn't identify the expression that flickered in Bart's eyes, but he definitely recognized her grandparents' names. "They were friends of Jeanette's mostly, but I liked them. How are they?"

"My grandmother retired and moved to Arizona after my grandfather passed away," Kaylee said.

The sympathy that washed over the man's face appeared genuine, and he murmured condolences, but Jeanette's brother wasn't nearly so compassionate. "Was Jeanette with that Corzo woman when you saw them?"

"She was," Kaylee said simply.

"And was the Corzo woman drunk?" he demanded.

"No," Kaylee answered. "Roz doesn't drink."

The scruffy man snorted his disbelief. Kaylee wondered briefly if she might have discovered why Jeanette got along so well with Roz. She had to be used to dealing with difficult people after having this man for a brother. Then she chastised herself for the uncharitable thought. *The poor guy may have lost his sister. He has a right to be a little cranky.*

"You still haven't said whether you're coming with us to the inn," Bart said to Kaylee.

"Ms. Bleu will be helping out in identifying the contents of some tea both Roz and Jeanette drank," Nick replied, which Kaylee noticed wasn't exactly an answer to the question, but Bart seemed to find the response adequate.

"Jeanette was always concocting different herbal tea mixes. Some of them were absolutely vile," he said. "I was almost afraid to tell her when I had a cold. She'd brew up the most disgusting 'cures.'"

"Who cares what was in a cup of tea?" Jeanette's brother huffed. "It wasn't tea that pitched my sister over the rail of a boat."

"We don't know what happened," Nick said, his voice still reasonable. Kaylee was impressed with his tolerance for the strangers' behavior. "Mrs. Corzo had a negative reaction to the tea. If your sister did as well, she could have become disoriented and fallen overboard."

"With the life raft Ms. Bleu mentioned? That's the stupidest thing I've ever heard!" Lyle roared. "It's clear to me that Roz threw my sister overboard, then pitched the duffel bag after her. And it's equally clear that you're searching for a way to get that woman off the hook. I'm not having it!"

As Lyle continued to bluster, Kaylee glanced toward Bart, who was nodding along with his brother-in-law. He might have better self-control, but he clearly blamed Roz every bit as much.

"We're merely searching for the truth," Nick tried to say over Lyle, his tone getting more forceful.

Kaylee realized that she would rather not be caught in the cross fire of hostility between these men as they discussed Jeanette's disappearance at the Northern Lights. "Excuse me," she cut in when Lyle paused for a breath. "Bear needs a walk, so I will pass on joining you at the inn. I doubt my botany expertise will be helpful there."

"Finally something I can agree with," the burly man growled.

Bart offered his hand again. "It was nice meeting you. Perhaps we will see one another again."

Kaylee shook his hand, then stepped away with real relief. She doubted Roz would agree that she'd done enough, but Kaylee was not up for any more drama. Once she was far enough from the men that Lyle Colson's angry voice didn't make her shoulders twitch, she set Bear down. "Back to the shop," she told him. "And I'll even give you a treat for not snapping at those cranky men."

Bear wagged his tail vigorously at the word *treat* and pointed his nose toward the route he knew so well. When they reached the sidewalk, Kaylee sensed someone approaching from the side. She spun to see the woman in the business suit, though now her wool coat was buttoned over it. Kaylee offered her a tentative smile.

"How do you do?" the woman said briskly. "I'm Margaret Olber. I'm Jeanette Colson's work supervisor." Her tone lightened. "Also her friend. I heard you talking to those men on the dock. Has something happened to Jeanette?"

Kaylee felt a knot forming in her stomach. No wonder police officers hated this portion of the job. "I'm sorry, but she's missing."

"Oh." The woman stood uncannily still.

Kaylee had no idea what to say so she simply waited. Her gaze drifted to Bear, who stood studying the woman curiously.

Finally a nerve twitched in the woman's cheek and she spoke again. "Jeanette told me she was coming to Orcas Island and I'd never been here, so she invited me along. I was tied up with some personal stuff, and I wasn't sure I was going to be able to come out at all. I couldn't join her until today." She blinked her eyes rapidly. "I'm not quite sure what to do."

Kaylee frowned, remembering Jeanette saying in Death by Chocolate that she was only staying on the island through the weekend. Why would she invite a coworker to join her if she didn't intend to stay?

"You should probably talk to Deputy Nick Durham," Kaylee finally managed, gesturing behind her to where he was still talking to Lyle and Bart. "He can answer your questions far better than I can. He is handling the investigation at this point."

The tall woman winced at the word *investigation*. "So the police believe something bad happened to Jeanette?"

"She was on a boat when she vanished," Kaylee explained. "In the middle of some rough water. She apparently had a raft with her, but using it in that weather would have been extremely unsafe. If she used the raft for some reason, it doesn't appear that she made it to shore."

"She was good with boats," Margaret said. "She said she

practically grew up on the water. Maybe she made it to the island and is lying low?"

"Would she have any reason for that?" Kaylee asked.

"Maybe. I got the impression she was fond of pranks." Margaret wrung her gloved hands. "This is all quite distressing."

Kaylee couldn't imagine anyone voluntarily stepping out of Roz's relatively safe boat and into a raft on a night like that, but was it her place to crush whatever hope the woman had? After all, they hadn't found anything definite yet. "Unfortunately I don't have much more information than you do. Deputy Durham is the person to talk to for details."

Margaret pursed her lips and gestured toward the ferry dock. "Maybe I'll wait until the deputy is done with those angry men. I hate to interrupt."

"I believe they are all going to the Northern Lights Inn to continue the discussion out of the cold," Kaylee said. "You might want to go there. I know they have hot coffee available."

The woman shivered. "That would be good." She peered closely at Kaylee. "Jeanette said she was coming out to the island to visit a friend. Was that you?"

"No, I only met Jeanette very briefly on Friday."

Margaret blinked, her expression confused. "Then how are you involved?"

"I wouldn't say I'm involved. I am a forensic botanist, and I'll be identifying some plant matter that is a tiny part of the investigation." She waved a hand toward the little dachshund at her feet. "I was walking Bear when the ferry came in. He loves visiting the dock and seeing all the new people." Though this wasn't exactly the full truth, Kaylee felt that Nick wouldn't want her to give out too much information to a stranger.

The tall woman smiled down at Bear. "He's a handsome dog, but he must be cold. Forgive me for keeping you. I'll go along to the inn. Could you point me in the right direction? Is it walkable from here?"

Relieved to be on less emotional ground, Kaylee quickly gave the woman directions. When she finished, the tall woman thanked her and hefted the strap of her bag slightly higher on her shoulder before marching off toward the inn.

Kaylee watched her walk away, then she and Bear headed for The Flower Patch. She'd be glad to get indoors since the cold felt as if it had crept into her bones. Unless it was simply the creepiness of the whole situation. How had Jeanette disappeared from Roz's boat? And where was she now?

As much as Kaylee wanted the answers to both questions, she had the lingering sense that once those answers were discovered, it wasn't going to be good news. Not for anyone.

5

The weather report promised more rain on Tuesday morning, so Kaylee was grateful to get to the shop before it started. The streets of Turtle Cove were practically empty as she drove in, and puddles dotted the low points of every sidewalk. The quiet wasn't overly strange in the early hours of the day. Still, Kaylee knew they weren't going to see many more visitors if additional rain was coming. "We could use a few nice days," she said to Bear as she parked.

Bear wagged his tail as if in agreement, and Kaylee chuckled. She suspected he was as tired of getting wet on their walks as she was. "Spring is coming," she assured him. *Not quickly, but it's coming.*

The air was cold but not windy, so Kaylee and Bear managed to make it all the way from the car to the shop's back door without either of them shivering. Water dripped from the porch roof and darkened the branches of bare trees, and everything smelled wet. Once inside, Bear shook vigorously, as if the damp air was enough to make him soggy.

"It's not raining already, is it?" Mary asked as she walked from the worktable to join them. She handed Kaylee a small towel they kept for drying wet paws.

"No," Kaylee said as she bent to wipe Bear's feet. "I think Bear is practicing." Bear lapped her hands as she wiped off his front paws, then when she was done, he trotted over to Mary, holding his head high as if to show off the white bow tie speckled with tiny kitten faces.

"You are very handsome," Mary assured him as she scratched

his ears. When she stood, she asked, "Did you get all the paperwork caught up?"

"Despite everything, yes."

"Despite everything?" Mary's voice was teasing. "Did Reese come by?"

"Reese is still on the mainland. I'm talking about Jeanette."

Mary's smile vanished. "What has that woman done now?"

"I can't believe you haven't heard." As a former dispatcher, Mary usually had her finger on the pulse of everything that happened in Turtle Cove. Kaylee quickly caught her up on the events of Monday, ending with mentioning the next step of the investigation that involved her. "Nick is coming by this morning so I can examine the dregs from the tea."

"I'm sure the sheriff's department appreciates having a skilled botanist at hand," Mary said, then she frowned. "But I don't think I like Roz demanding that you poke around in an ongoing investigation, especially if Jeanette's brother is as antagonistic as he sounds. You could end up in danger."

"I'm not afraid of Lyle," Kaylee said, being mostly truthful. "But Roz *is* afraid. She's terrified the police are going to listen to Lyle and Bart and arrest her. Plus all the talk about her drinking has hurt her feelings."

"I don't know why I'd even try suggesting you not investigate, but do be careful, Kaylee. If someone did hurt Jeanette—or worse—that person won't want you poking around."

"At this point, I am simply going to analyze some tea leaves at the behest of the sheriff's department. But first, I'm making coffee. Do you want some?"

"I always want coffee."

With the boost of caffeine, Mary and Kaylee busied themselves as best they could that morning. A few regulars came into the shop, risking the darkening sky for flowers to brighten the gloom, but most of the next few hours went by quietly—aside from the pitter-patter of rain that fell on the roof with growing intensity.

Shortly before noon, the bell on the shop's front door announced Nick's arrival. He'd barely made it onto the sales floor before Bear leaped up from his cushion behind the front counter and rushed over to greet him, yapping excitedly.

"Hi buddy," Nick said, reaching down to pet Bear's silky head. He straightened and flashed a winning smile at Kaylee and Mary. "Good morning, ladies."

"Hi Nick," Kaylee said. "Do you have the samples?"

"You're getting right down to business," Nick said. "Must be a slow day."

"I think it's slow everywhere on Orcas Island," Mary said with a sigh. "Except the sheriff's office, apparently."

"Apparently." Nick pulled a bulky manila envelope from beneath his sheriff's department-issue rain slicker. "I'm ready when you are, Kaylee."

"You can hang your jacket on the coatrack, then let's head upstairs." Kaylee glanced down at Bear. "Bear, stay. You can get more pets from your favorite deputy in a little while."

After Nick removed his coat, Kaylee led the way up to the experimental growing room where she kept her microscope. She unlocked and opened the door, then flicked on the bright overhead lights.

Nick dug into his evidence bag and removed a pair of clear vials bearing handwritten labels. "These are the dregs I collected from the mugs. Can you confirm whether both of them drank the same tea and identify what was in it?"

"I'll do my best." Kaylee took the vials from Nick and set about preparing slides. As she worked, she glanced sideways at Nick, who was perched on a tall stool nearby. "Did you ever talk to Margaret Olber?"

"You met her?" he asked.

Kaylee carefully swirled the contents of one of the vials, holding it up to let the light shine through. "I did. She came up to me right after I left you with Jeanette's brother and ex-husband."

"Margaret Olber holds a fairly high position in the company where she and Jeanette work," Nick said. "I thought she was an unusual woman to hold such a spot. She seemed very nervous. Almost timid. Normally people in the higher job slots are a little more assertive and confident."

"Maybe she's incredibly good at her job," Kaylee suggested as she gently plucked a bit of matter from one of the vials with sterile tweezers and set it on a glass slide.

"I suppose." Nick's tone was dubious.

Kaylee placed the fresh slide onto the microscope platform. "Did she tell you anything useful about Jeanette?"

"She said Jeanette had been unusually quiet at work lately," Nick said. "Almost depressed. Ms. Olber said she hoped the trip to the island to visit an old friend would cheer her up."

Kaylee glanced up from the microscope in surprise. "She said Jeanette was depressed? She certainly didn't seem depressed when I saw her on Friday."

Nick shrugged. "Maybe visiting Roz worked."

"Can you imagine a visit to Roz helping you overcome depression?" Kaylee asked.

Nick's lip twitched, and Kaylee suspected he was stifling a laugh. "Not for me, no. It takes all kinds of people to fill the world, though."

"I suppose." Kaylee returned her attention to the microscope.

"Now for my question," Nick said. "Did she tell *you* anything interesting about Jeanette?"

Kaylee delicately adjusted the focus on the microscope. "She said Jeanette had invited her to come out to the island, which is odd since Jeanette had said she was only staying through the weekend. She also said Jeanette was very good with boats. That's about all."

"I talked to Roz," Nick said. "She told me Jeanette never mentioned a friend joining them."

"Margaret did say that she wasn't sure she'd be able to come. Maybe Jeanette wasn't expecting her to make it, so she'd decided on a shorter visit. That might explain the conflicting information."

"Maybe."

The conversation fell off as Kaylee studied the plant material under the slide and began running a few tests while Nick waited patiently, though he did finally pull out his phone. He held the screen away from her, and she suspected he'd resorted to playing games to pass the time.

Finally Kaylee knew as much as she was going to learn. "The ingredients are primarily a mix of herbs. Most are about what I'd expect to find in an herbal tea: chamomile, catnip, fennel seed, rose hips, lavender, and spearmint."

"Catnip?" Nick asked. "People drink tea with catnip in it?"

"It's not uncommon. But what is uncommon was the last ingredient I found. There were valerian leaves and dried, ground valerian root. A lot of it. Far more than I'd expect to find in a normal tea, and more than enough to make the tea taste bitter and horrible. It's no wonder Roz said it was disgusting." She held out the tiny vial toward Nick. "Sniff this."

He held up his hands. "I caught a whiff when I collected it. I don't need to relive it. Smells like dirty socks."

Kaylee nodded. "That's how the scent of dried valerian root is often described. But that smell wouldn't normally be nearly so strong. No one would put that much of the stuff in something they were going to drink. Plus, the second vial has only a few bits of valerian leaf, but no dried root. So the cup this came from wouldn't be as strong or taste as bad."

"So what exactly does this stuff do?" Nick asked.

"Valerian has a sedative effect. It is used as a sleep aid. And some holistic vets offer valerian drops that calm pets who are afraid of storms. In this kind of concentration, though, I'm surprised it didn't make Roz sick."

"So Jeanette knocked Roz out on purpose," Nick mused.

"Normally it wouldn't knock someone out. It has a sedative effect, but not enough to use it that way. In these concentrations, it would make a person drowsy though, assuming the drinker could keep the stuff down. I'd expect it to leave her with a headache as well."

"But Roz said she passed out. Are you saying she lied?"

"Not necessarily. She told me she hadn't slept much the night before. With the addition of that kind of exhaustion, it's possible it would have had the effect she described."

"So where do you get that root stuff?" Nick asked.

"Roz said Jeanette made her own tea," Kaylee said. "And all of the plants are fairly easy to grow, even valerian. *Valeriana officinalis* is a perennial that bears little white or pink flowers and grows quite tall, normally around four or five feet. The stink comes from the root only. The flowers actually smell quite pleasant, almost like vanilla."

"Does anyone on the island grow it?"

"Not that I've heard," Kaylee said. "This time of year, you certainly couldn't find it outside of a greenhouse."

"What if I wanted to buy local herbal tea, or even just loose herbs? Where would I find it?"

"I think I've seen an herbal tea shop in Eastsound. You might ask some questions there."

"Suppose I happened to have one of those valerian plants

growing in my house in a sunny spot. How would I make it into tea?"

"First, the plant requires a lot of sun," Kaylee said. "And they're spindly and tall, and the plants tend to spread. So growing one indoors would take some doing."

"Let's imagine I pulled it off."

"You'd dig up the roots and rinse them. They're hairy and thin. You'd probably want to spread all those roots out on a screen in a dehydrator and dry them out. The more they dry, the more they'll smell. Then after a few hours, you'd grind up the root with a mortar and pestle, and you'd be ready to add it to tea or fill capsules with it."

"Thanks," Nick said. "That's very helpful."

"Does this prove that Roz wasn't at fault in Jeanette's disappearance?" Kaylee asked. "Roz would hardly have knocked herself out."

"We only have Roz's word on which mug was hers at this point. Both mugs had prints from both women, and we won't have DNA evidence anytime soon, as that had to be sent to the mainland. It's not impossible that Roz drugged Jeanette to make it easier to pitch her overboard."

"You can't believe that."

"I don't. But I can't rule it out."

"I've never seen Roz show much interest in plants," Kaylee said. "And she certainly is no fan of herbal tea, so it seems unlikely she'd choose this method. Plus, Jeanette was fairly tall, but Roz is both bigger and bulkier. If Roz wanted to pitch the woman off the boat, she could invite her out onto the deck and strong-arm her over."

"Kaylee, I don't have it out for Roz," Nick said. "But I can't just blindly give her a pass either, not if I'm going to do my job right. Thank you for your help with the tea, though."

"You're welcome," Kaylee said, but she still wished she'd been able to find something that cleared Roz. The boat captain had never been exactly friendly, but she'd been a fixture around town ever since Kaylee had arrived. She wanted her to be innocent.

The day began to crawl after Nick left, and Kaylee and Mary had to search for ways to stay busy. Early afternoon found Kaylee tidying the ribbon rack behind the front counter while Mary cleaned up the kitchen from their leisurely lunch. When the bell over the door jingled its merry sound, an expectant Kaylee spun around to see that the visitor was Roz, who stood shaking off the rain onto the doormat.

"I was hoping the rain had stopped," Kaylee said.

"I bet we've got a few more hours of it at the very least." Roz walked closer to the counter and smacked both hands down on it. "You learn anything about Jeanette's disappearance?"

Instead of answering the question, Kaylee responded with one of her own. "What do you know about the tea you drank?"

Roz wrinkled her nose. "It tasted disgusting. Jeanette was crazy about that stuff. Always had been."

"And she said she made it?"

Roz nodded her head so vigorously that drops of water landed on the counter. "She's always made her own tea. Even when she lived here, she was crazy into herbalism. She even hung out with Smith Hooper, and that guy is creepy."

"Smith Hooper?" Kaylee echoed. "I've never heard that name."

Roz crossed her arms over her chest. "That's a surprise. You'd think you two would be best friends since he grows all kinds of weeds on his property to make tea out of."

"What does he do with the tea?" Kaylee asked.

"Sells it." This remark came from Mary who emerged from the kitchen to join them. She had two cups of coffee in her hands, and she gave one to Kaylee. "He supplies a shop in Eastsound."

Roz looked eagerly at the coffee and Kaylee simply handed her the mug Mary had given her. "What kind of shop?" Kaylee asked as Roz took a noisy slurp.

"One of those nutty crystals-and-weeds tea shops," Roz said, lowering the mug. "It's got some flaky name, Life Balance or something."

"Balanced Life," Mary said. "I only went in there once. It's a bit too new age for me. The window is full of tie-dyed T-shirts in tourist season. Not that I have anything against the shirts, mind you. A woman from church makes them, and she says the shop does a brisk business."

"Does Smith Hooper sell his stuff anywhere here in Turtle Cove?" Kaylee asked. Perfectly Natural, the organic grocery store managed by Andy Wilcox, carried herbal tea, but she seemed to remember it being a national brand.

"He used to sell tea at the farmers market," Mary said. "But Smith isn't exactly good at interacting with people."

Roz hooted with laughter, nearly spilling her coffee. "Not good with people? Smith makes me look like a social butterfly. The man is a hermit and a kook."

"But he knows Jeanette?" Kaylee asked.

Roz nodded. "Jeanette was about the only person I ever knew who could make that man act friendly. She can charm a rock."

Kaylee cocked her head. "Can you tell me where he lives?"

"Of course." Roz gave her directions, which Kaylee scribbled on a notepad on the counter. It sounded more than a little convoluted. "I hope you're planning on doing more than talking to Smith. I need you squelching that rotten rumor about me drinking. I keep hearing that one." Roz huffed. "Maybe if folks start talking about Smith's tea, they'll stop talking about the drinking problem *I don't have*." She smacked the coffee mug down on the counter with that remark, then spun and tromped out into the rain.

"Roz is pretty worked up about all this," Mary observed as she wiped the counter where coffee had sloshed out of the mug. "Do you want me to get you some coffee of your own?"

"You're sweet to offer, but I can get it." Kaylee stepped out from behind the counter. Bear hopped up from his napping spot to follow her. "I'm not exactly fending off a mob of customers."

"Maybe when the rain stops." Mary walked to the kitchen with Kaylee and Bear. The little dog glanced wistfully toward the closest exit.

"Sorry Bear," Kaylee said. "We'll go out as soon as the rain lets up."

The little dog sighed and flopped down next to the small kitchen table.

"He has the right idea," Mary said. "We should hibernate until spring."

"These gray days do make that appealing," Kaylee agreed as she rinsed Roz's mug in the sink. "If the rain stops, I might go ahead and drive out to chat with Smith Hooper. This whole business with the tea is confusing. Why would Jeanette want to drug Roz with tea?"

"I can think of one reason," Mary said. "Maybe she didn't want Roz awake because Roz would try to stop her from doing something bad."

Kaylee poured coffee into the clean mug and nodded. "I think you're right that Jeanette wanted Roz out of the way because she planned to do something Roz wouldn't approve of."

"But what?"

"I'm thinking smuggling or something nefarious," Kaylee said. "Something she wouldn't want Roz to witness."

"In that case, where is she?" Mary asked. "She wasn't on the boat, which means she either left it voluntarily or she was removed against her will. Which do you think it was?"

"I couldn't say. Maybe the deal went wrong." Kaylee sank into one of the kitchen chairs. "It feels like all I have right now are questions." She set her mug on the table, then fixed her gaze on Mary. "But I plan to get some answers."

6

After the rain finally stopped, Kaylee waited a while longer in case the deluge of precipitation was replaced by a deluge of customers, but only one browser came in. "I think I should go talk to Smith Hooper," Kaylee said to Mary as soon as their sole customer left with a small bag of goat-milk soap. "If I leave now, I may be able to get out to his place before dark. Would you mind closing today?"

Mary walked around the counter to neaten the soap display. "I certainly should be able to handle the crowd. Do you want me to watch Bear too? I could take him home for some time in front of the television with Herb."

Snagging Bear's leash from the coatrack, Kaylee said, "Thanks, but I'll bring him with me. Bear can be a great ambassador." As she bent to attach the leash to his collar, she scratched him under the chin. "After all, who could resist that face?" Bear's tail wagged furiously at the compliment.

"No argument on that," Mary said. "You be careful though. Smith is a little strange."

Kaylee straightened up, her attention on her friend. "Strange enough to kill Jeanette?"

"I don't think so, but I've been wrong about people before."

"Haven't we all?" Kaylee gave Mary a quick hug. "Thanks for closing for me. I promise to be careful."

She led Bear out into the gray February afternoon. The rain had dropped the temperature a few more degrees, and Kaylee clutched the lapels of her coat close around her neck as she walked to the car. The little dog squinted against the cold breeze and seemed grateful once they were tucked into the vehicle with the heater blasting.

While the car warmed up, Kaylee studied the directions for a few minutes, frowning at all the turns. She thought she knew her way around Turtle Cove, but she wasn't aware that some of these roads even existed. "Well, Bear," she said, trying to sound upbeat, "this should be an adventure."

Bear didn't respond, and Kaylee hoped that wasn't an omen for the errand ahead. After a number of turns, she found herself on a bumpy road scored with potholes that wound through trees and brush and not much else.

"It seems to me that Smith Hooper might be a hermit whether he wanted to be or not," Kaylee said aloud. "I doubt he'd get a lot of guests when the way to his house is this rough. I think if you fell into any of these potholes, you might have trouble climbing out."

With trees on both sides of the road blocking the light, the afternoon gloom quickly changed to near darkness, which didn't help in navigating the treacherous road. Kaylee finally decided that the directions must be wrong and began searching for a place wide enough to turn around, but the road wasn't simply rough, it was narrow as well, with trees growing close on either side.

The car bumped around a corner and Kaylee found herself facing a tall, weathered Victorian house. Plants encroached on the house from all sides, with vines and bushes actually covering some of the windows completely. A well-lit conservatory jutted out on one side like a strange, glowing growth, and Kaylee wondered if that might be where the man grew his herbs. The way it blazed with light suggested it was the best place to find Smith Hooper.

She hopped out of her car and scooped up Bear, then walked to the conservatory's ornate exterior door. Though the glass was far from clean, she could see movement inside. Suddenly nervous of bringing Bear into the building, she gently put him down and looped his leash over the door handle. "I think it might be best if you stay here. You're out of the wind, and I promise to be back soon."

Bear whined quietly, clearly not appreciating the signs that he was going to be left behind.

"It's okay, big guy," Kaylee murmured. "I'll be quick. In fact, I might be thrown out immediately. But I won't forget you're here."

Hot, moist air hit Kaylee's face as she opened the door enough to slip through. She squeezed through the crack and saw that no plants were growing close to the door, so she left it ajar. That way, Bear could see her inside and benefit from the warmth emanating from within. Bear preferred to be able to see her, and she didn't plan to be inside long enough for the cold coming back in to be a problem for any delicate plants inside.

She walked to the first of a long row of racks, all with trays of small plants on each shelf. Down the row, she spotted a white-haired man kneeling beside the bottom shelf of one rack. He seemed to be thinning a collection of tiny, delicate plants.

"Mr. Hooper?" Kaylee said tentatively.

The man jumped to his feet, an easy movement that belied the white hair on his head. Kaylee saw then that he was a few inches shorter than she was.

"What are you doing on my property?" the man roared at her, waving his hands.

"I don't mean to intrude," Kaylee said, taking an involuntary step back.

"Then you shouldn't trespass!" the man shouted.

Apparently his fiercely angry voice carried because Kaylee heard Bear barking from outside, adding to the din the herbalist made as he bellowed at her.

"Calm down, please. I'll go," Kaylee promised, struggling to be heard over the herbalist's continued hollering.

Did Bear's barking sound louder? *Oh no! Bear must have gotten loose.* Kaylee risked turning her back on the angry older man in order to catch her dog. She didn't *think* he would bite the man simply for yelling, but it was a risk she didn't intend to take.

Bear skidded around the corner and raced toward Smith Hooper, barking and growling as he came. As worried as Kaylee was, she almost chuckled at her tiny guardian, who rushed bravely to her defense. She crouched to catch him before he could get by her.

To her surprise, she realized Mr. Hooper had fallen silent. She twisted to look at him, giving Bear the opportunity to zip past her.

"Well, hello there," the herbalist said, his face wreathed by a huge grin.

Bear stopped, clearly not sure if the man in front of him was friend or foe.

"Bear, come," Kaylee commanded.

The little dog peered at her, then at the herbalist, obviously confused about whether he was supposed to say hi or defend Kaylee.

Mr. Hooper sank down on one knee. "It's all right," he said to Bear, reaching out with a gnarled hand. "I wasn't going to hurt your friend. I didn't realize she traveled in such distinguished company."

A dog lover! Relief rushed through Kaylee as she took a tentative step forward. "I'm Kaylee Bleu. I own The Flower Patch."

He blinked at her. "Kaylee? You're Bea and Ed's granddaughter?"

Kaylee's own smile widened. "I am. And this is Bear."

The older man beamed down at the little dog again. "My late wife loved dachshunds. Wonderful little dogs. We always had one."

Bear closed the distance between himself and Mr. Hooper, then sniffed the man's outstretched hand before relenting and letting the herbalist pat him on the head.

"You don't have one now?" Kaylee asked.

The man's expression fell. "It wouldn't be right without Anna." He scratched Bear's ears. "But I do enjoy seeing your Bear. He's a brave one."

"He is that," Kaylee agreed. "And I'm sorry for barging in on you."

The man waved away her apology. "That's all right. You surprised me, that's all. And I've forgotten my manners over the years." He gave her a sad smile. "My Anna would be appalled. Did you come in search of herbs?"

"Not so much herbs as information," Kaylee said.

"I can do that too. I've been studying herbs nearly all my life, though the world of plants is so vast, I'm sure there are still surprises they can teach me." He gestured toward the other end of the conservatory. "I have a thermos of tea. Would you care for some? I make it myself."

"That sounds lovely," Kaylee said, though she wasn't entirely certain she should drink the man's tea considering what she'd found in the dregs from the boat. Still, she didn't want to offend him, not after Bear had softened him up. She decided to at least pretend she was drinking the tea he offered.

She followed the man through the rows of plant racks until they came to an old cast-iron bistro set. Though paint was flaking off the ornate scrollwork of the table and chairs, they were still beautiful. The older man gestured toward one of the two chairs and placed a delicate china cup and saucer before her. "I can drink out of the cap from the thermos," he said. "I'm not properly prepared for guests."

"I shouldn't have come unannounced," Kaylee said apologetically, "but I didn't have any other way to contact you."

"That's perfectly all right. I don't answer the phone half the time. I suppose I've grown attached to my solitude." Mr. Hooper opened a tall thermos and poured tea into the china cup. The tea steamed slightly, despite the warm air in the conservatory. Then he poured tea in the thermos lid and took a long sip before setting the tea down. "Now, how can I help you?"

"I actually wanted to ask you about someone you know. Jeanette Colson? She has disappeared, and I thought you might be able to help me understand her better."

"Disappeared?" Mr. Hooper's expression grew alarmed. "Perhaps she simply left the island again. I believe she was only visiting for a few days. Don't tell me she ran out on her hotel bill or something equally unsavory. Jeanette was always rather impulsive."

"She vanished from a boat," Kaylee said. "And some herbal tea was involved."

Alarm transitioned into confusion on the older man's face. "Tea was involved in her disappearance?"

"It's all a little vague. I'm sorry that I can't tell you more, but someone mentioned to me that Jeanette learned about herbs from you."

"Yes." His voice was serious as he spoke. "Jeanette had a passion for herbs and their medical uses. She reminded me of my Anna that way, so I agreed to teach her. That was years ago, and she didn't stay to learn everything I could teach. When her marriage fell apart, she fled the island without even saying goodbye."

"That must have hurt," Kaylee said as she held the delicate cup in her hand and swirled the golden tea gently.

"It did. More than a little." Mr. Hooper sighed. "I wasn't exactly happy to see her the other day."

"So she did come out here."

He nodded. "She told me she'd given up growing and drying her own herbs. Apparently she lives in a small apartment in the city, though she told me that she plans to move to a bigger place where she can grow plants again. I thought she might have said that because she could see I was disappointed in her. Jeanette was once quite gifted with plants and remedies."

Kaylee wondered if Jeanette was talking about her possible reconnection with Bart. She made a mental note to ask if he lived in an apartment or a house. "So Jeanette's visit was social?"

"Partly, I suppose, but she came to buy some tea."

Kaylee set the cup down on the saucer. "Tea with valerian?"

"Yes," Mr. Hooper said. "The tea I sold her includes a small amount of valerian leaf, which offers a soothing effect along with the chamomile. The leaves of the valerian plant have a much milder sedative effect than the roots, and they both smell and taste better."

"There was no valerian root in the tea?" Kaylee asked.

He gaped at her in surprise. "No, none. The tea I sold her was meant to be soothing, so I mixed it to have a pleasant flavor. Valerian root has a very strong taste. Not many would consume it unless they were specifically seeking out its sedative effects. I sell nearly all my valerian root to a holistic veterinarian on the mainland."

Kaylee glanced around. "But you do grow it?"

"In warmer weather, I have a patch outside." Mr. Hooper gestured toward the closest window. "During the cold months, I grow some in here. It can be quite challenging to keep up with demand during the winter as the vet sells a lot of valerian root. It's great for calming dogs who are afraid of storms, and you'd be amazed at how many of those there are." He peered over the table at Bear. "I doubt your protector is astraphobic."

"He's too brave for that," Kaylee agreed, still pondering what the herbalist had said. "Could you tell me exactly what plants were in the tea you sold Jeanette?"

Mr. Hooper seemed to appraise her for a moment before he answered. "Chamomile, catnip, fennel seed, rose hips, lavender, valerian leaf, and spearmint. It's a mild calming blend."

"And she didn't buy any valerian root on top of it?"

He shook his head. "She asked me about it, but this time of year I have trouble meeting demand, so I didn't have any to spare. Valerian is not a plant that thrives when grown in a pot. It requires a lot of light, and the roots tend to be leggy. The plant spreads quickly when grown in an outdoor bed."

"Would she know where you grow your valerian plants in here?" Kaylee asked.

"Of course. At one time Jeanette knew this conservatory as well as I do, and I don't change my layout. I'm a creature of habit. My wife often teased me about it."

Kaylee scooted slightly forward on her chair, her hands resting on Bear's back. "Would you be willing to show me the plants?"

"Of course," he said, his expression curious. He stood. "I can take you now, since it doesn't seem that you're actually going to drink that tea."

Kaylee felt her cheeks warm. "I'm sorry. I'm sure it's lovely."

Smith chuckled. "No need to apologize. Herbal tea isn't for everyone."

Kaylee picked up the end of Bear's leash and stood, then followed the herbalist down a row of plants.

"I have to put the containers for the large plants back here," Mr. Hooper said as they walked. "They take up so much room, and the valerian especially requires extra grow lights."

At the end of the long row of racks, they came into a more open space. A series of large pots stood in a group under bright lights. In all but one of the pots, tall plants with thin stems and pretty pale-pink blooms seemed to strain toward the lights. Kaylee caught the slightly sweet scent from the flowers. Bear must have smelled it too, as he suddenly sneezed in her arms.

"What is this?" Smith stormed over to the one empty pot.

Kaylee hurried along behind him and spotted an uprooted

valerian plant sprawled on the floor, its branches and blossoms wilted. Even Kaylee could see that someone had chopped off the plant's roots. She put a hand to her cheek, horrified. "Could Jeanette have done this?"

"She would certainly be aware of how important this plant is to my business." The herbalist knelt by the plant and gathered up what was left of it, cradling it gently in his hands like a pet. "I can't believe she would do such a thing. If she truly needed the valerian, she should have told me. I would never have refused her if I'd thought she was desperate enough to do *this*."

"I'm so sorry," Kaylee said. "Is there anything I can do?"

He shook his head. "If I'd found this sooner, I might have been able to take cuttings and root them, but it was left on the cold, dry floor too long. It's completely dead." He stood slowly, the plant still in his hands. "Can you see yourself out? I've got to clean this up and check on my other plants."

"Of course," Kaylee said. "Again, I'm sorry." She reached into her purse and pulled out a business card. "I'll leave this on the table where we had tea. If you find anything else Jeanette might have done, would you please call me?"

"Of course." Mr. Hooper never glanced up from the ruined plant in his hands, but his voice cracked a little as he said, "It's the waste that bothers me. Jeanette should value plants more than this. I taught her better. I thought . . ." He stopped and shook his head sadly before walking past Kaylee and disappearing down the closest row.

"We'd best get home," Kaylee told Bear, then dropped off the business card and led her dog through the cold to the car.

As they drove back to Wildflower Cottage, Kaylee thought about what she'd learned in the herbalist's conservatory. It was fairly obvious that Jeanette had stolen the valerian root from Mr. Hooper. But how could she have used it on Roz so quickly?

Valerian root had to be dried before it could be ingested. So if Jeanette had stolen the root directly from the herbalist's plant, how had she dried it for use in the tea? Had she brought a dehydrator to the island?

Kaylee sighed. She may have gotten an answer or two, but now she had even more questions than before.

On Wednesday morning, Kaylee was delighted to find the sky clear and the temperature slightly warmer. "This is promising," she told Bear as they set off for work. As the road to downtown Turtle Cove curved along the water, Kaylee's thoughts turned to the water as well—more specifically, to the woman who had disappeared while boating on it five days earlier.

"We know how Jeanette got the valerian," Kaylee said to Bear. "But it still makes no sense that she'd want to knock her friend out while they were out on rough water."

Bear didn't answer, instead focusing his attention on a swooping seagull.

"I think we should check with Roz," Kaylee continued. "Maybe she can tell us where Jeanette was staying and how she might have been able to dry that root. I think Mary will forgive us if we're a tiny bit late."

She aimed her car toward the marina where Roz kept her boat. To her surprise, when she and Bear walked down the wharf, they found the slip empty. Kaylee stared at the lapping water, wondering where Roz might be.

"You hunting for Roz Corzo?"

Kaylee squinted up at the boat that was moored in the next slip. A grizzled man in a thick canvas coat peered down at her.

The low angle of the sun made it shine over the man's shoulder and right into Kaylee's eyes. She put up a hand to shield her eyes. "I am. Have you seen her?"

The gray head bobbed. "She took some deputies out on the water." He cackled. "I reckon she was showing them where she dumped the body."

As she watched the man laugh at his own questionable sense of humor, Kaylee remembered Roz and Jeanette's conversation in the bakery. "Are you Pop Ronson?"

The man was clearly surprised that Kaylee had called him by name, but he gave her a cocky grin. "I guess my fame is spreading."

"I heard you had a disagreement with Roz."

The man laughed again. "Have you ever met her? The woman is a walking argument. Everyone has had a disagreement with her at one time or another."

Kaylee didn't really have anything to say to that, so she changed the subject. "Did you meet her friend Jeanette?"

"I did, briefly. She seemed nice enough. Not the old grouch that Roz always is."

"Did you ever witness them fighting?" Kaylee asked, though she immediately felt disloyal to Roz for the question.

The boat captain shook his head. "No, though I heard Roz grumble at her more than once. I'd have never figured those two for friends. Oil and water, they were. Roz is always spoiling for a fight, and that other one was perky all the time."

"Did you see them Friday night?"

"I heard Corzo's tub go chugging out into the night for that little tea party they had. I remember thinking that was a foolish thing to do. I thought Corzo had better sense than that."

Kaylee latched on to the remark about a tea party. She was surprised that Pop had brought up the tea since the prevailing theory was apparently that Roz had been imbibing. So why would this man, who had a clear grudge against Roz, mention that it was tea they'd been drinking? It seemed unlikely that Roz had confided in him. "What makes you think they were drinking tea?"

His eyes narrowed. "What kind of stupid question is that? I've got work to do. I don't have time to spend yapping about those women." He disappeared before Kaylee could respond.

Kaylee stared up at Pop's boat, wondering at his sudden departure. Bear must have sensed that their errand had come to an end, because he strained on the leash, pulling Kaylee back toward her car.

"Right," she said as she followed him. "No more answers here. We'd best get on to work." As she let him lead her to the car, Kaylee wondered about the mysterious Mr. Ronson. If he knew about Jeanette's tea, what else might the man know?

7

"You've been holding that same daisy for five minutes," Mary said as she leaned against the doorway of the workroom. Near Mary's ankles, Bear peeked into the room as well. "It's going to wilt from your body heat if you don't decide what to do with it."

Kaylee stared at her friend, then at the daisy she held. With a laugh, she snapped out of it and slid the flower into the small arrangement she was working on. Mary had volunteered to take Bear for a walk, and Kaylee hadn't even noticed them return. "I was thinking about how distraught Smith Hooper was about his valerian plant. Jeanette would have known better than anyone how he felt about plants. How could she have been so callous?" She glanced down at Bear as he walked into the room only to collapse at her feet, leaning on her right ankle. "The plants are like his pets. He cares about them deeply."

"Maybe she was desperate," Mary suggested. "Or maybe it wasn't her. Valerian root can be sold as medicine. Someone could have stolen it for the money."

"In that case, why not take it all? There were a number of pots, but only one was disturbed."

"Maybe the thief was interrupted? Or maybe someone got lost out there and took advantage of the moment."

Kaylee considered that briefly, then shook her head. "I can't see anyone bumping down the road to his place by accident, never mind someone who'd be familiar enough with valerian to steal the roots. The thief must have gone out to his house intentionally."

"Maybe someone with a grudge. Smith isn't exactly genial."

"Again, I would expect someone like that to destroy more than a single plant."

"Roz knew about Smith Hooper." Mary crossed her arms over her chest. "And where he lived. She could have followed Jeanette out there and then grabbed the valerian root while Jeanette talked to Smith."

"I'm not sure Roz would recognize the plant," Kaylee said. "And it wasn't exactly out in the open with labels. Plus, I don't see Roz doing anything so sneaky. She's more the sort to punch a guy in the nose and take his stuff right in front of him if she felt the situation warranted it."

"I'll give you that. Roz has always been a direct person."

Kaylee spun the small arrangement in front of her, checking that all the flowers were in place. She was pleased to see that her distraction hadn't caused her to mess up the balance. "I think this will be the last arrangement I do today. We should have enough to get us through tomorrow."

"We didn't do too badly today," Mary said. "I was nearly bowled over by the rush at lunchtime."

Her friend's overstatement made Kaylee smile. Three women had come in during their lunch break from one of the small office buildings in Eastsound. They'd each bought an arrangement to brighten their desks.

"I was a little surprised they came so far," Kaylee said.

Mary shrugged. "I think they were having lunch at The Sunfish Café. I'm sure they were taking advantage of the first decent day we've had in a while. It makes me want to roam a little too."

"Well, then I think you should. Bear and I can handle the rest of today, even if we do get one last rush. It's only a few hours. Go on and have a ramble. And don't forget, you have tomorrow off. No rushing in and working. You're becoming a workaholic."

Kaylee carried her arrangement past Mary toward the sales floor, and Bear trotted along behind her.

"Takes one to know one," Mary teased as she followed Kaylee. "But I will take you up on the afternoon off. Not to shop, though. Instead, I'm going to rush home and clean."

Kaylee laughed in surprise. "You sound awfully excited about it."

"Only because Herb won't be there. He has an appointment at the barbershop in Eastsound, and he always spends hours there gossiping. So I'll be able to clean without him following me around offering to help but making it worse. Plus, by cleaning today, I'll be able to shop guilt-free tomorrow."

Mary gathered her things to leave and Kaylee enjoyed seeing the pleasure on her friend's face. Mary loved working at The Flower Patch as much as Kaylee, but the slow days they'd had lately did make the time drag a little.

After Mary left, Bear settled down behind the counter for a nap and Kaylee began sweeping the large main room. The slight uptick in traffic during the day had brought quite a bit of the outdoors in onto the floors, and Kaylee removed it with an optimistic energy. She hoped the warmer, busier day marked the beginning of a more bustling time at the shop. She didn't worry about income—she carefully budgeted for the slower winter months—but she looked forward to the challenge of having more work.

As she swept, she wondered if that might be part of why Roz's situation wouldn't leave her head. It was a challenge, something to pick apart and figure out. Plus, Kaylee was growing fascinated by the bundle of contradictions she was beginning to see in Jeanette. The woman had been lively and laughing on Friday, but she might also have torn up a plant belonging to a friend. She seemed fond of Roz, but she may have drugged her.

And she certainly had some extreme people in her life, if her brother was any example.

Once the dust and bits of dried mud were piled up in front of the counter, Kaylee reached over to snag the dustpan from where she'd left it. As she did, the front door opened, bringing a gust of wind from outside to scatter her neat pile. Kaylee scowled and spun to face the newcomer.

As he closed the door, Nick had the decency to look sheepishly at the broom in Kaylee's hand and the scattered dirt. "Sorry about that."

"It's all right, but if you don't mind, I'll get it swept into the pan before anyone else can open the door."

Nick stepped over to pick up the dustpan while Kaylee swept up the debris again. "I wanted to ask if you'd heard anything else about Jeanette's disappearance," he said, kneeling to hold the pan in place.

Kaylee scooted the dirt into it. "What makes you think I might?"

"Experience." Nick stood and handed her the pan. "Once you're curious, you seem to stay in the middle of things."

"Now you're making me sound intrusive." She walked around the counter and dumped the dust in the small trash can with vigor brought on by annoyance. Did everyone in Turtle Cove think she was meddlesome and pushy?

He held up his hands. "No insult intended. Can we call a truce?"

Kaylee sighed. "Sorry. I'm still smarting from Roz calling me nosy. Granted, I guess I have been nosy. I drove out to chat with Smith Hooper, an herbalist who apparently taught Jeanette all about herbal teas. It seems she bought the tea that she made for Roz there."

Nick raised his eyebrows. "Roz's statement said that Jeanette grew the herbs and made the tea herself."

"Apparently that's what Jeanette told Roz, but it's not true according to Smith Hooper," Kaylee said. "And I saw something else. Someone had pulled up one of his valerian plants to get at the roots. He thought it had to be Jeanette since she'd wanted to buy some valerian root, but he told her that all that he had was committed to a veterinarian customer. He was very upset about the destruction of his plant."

"That is interesting. I'll follow up with him."

"You might also want to check out wherever Jeanette was staying. Valerian root is used dried. It only takes a few hours to dry in a dehydrator, so you should see if she had one of those."

"We've searched her room at the Northern Lights," Nick said. "No dehydrator. She had bought a box fan though, which is a little odd this time of year. I thought she might use it for white noise when she slept. Some people do."

"Anything else odd?" Kaylee asked, suspecting the expression on Nick's face meant there was more he hadn't shared.

"Several furnace filters were leaning against the wall in one corner of the room."

"That *is* odd."

Nick shrugged. "I suppose she could have found a deal on them and meant to take them home."

"She lives in an apartment," Kaylee reminded him. "You don't usually need to provide furnace filters for a rental."

"Well, we'll sort it out eventually," Nick said. "But at least we've found out where the tea originated."

"And what Smith said supports Roz's statement," Kaylee pointed out. "That the tea was Jeanette's idea."

"The tea, sure," Nick agreed. "But Roz had been friends with Jeanette for a long time. She knew about her interest in herbalism, and maybe Roz picked up some facts about it from

Jeanette through the years. Maybe Roz followed Jeanette to the herbalist and saw an opportunity."

Kaylee hated the fact that Nick was echoing a line of thought Mary had brought up. Apparently Roz's innocence wasn't as obvious to everyone as it seemed to Kaylee. "Why are you even entertaining the idea that Roz killed an old friend?"

The deputy leaned on the counter on his elbows. "You know I have to entertain every idea, at least until we find the woman. And I heard Roz and Jeanette weren't always so friendly."

"They weren't?"

"Oh, do I have information you don't?" Nick grinned at her. "That's always a surprise."

Kaylee folded her arms and frowned at Nick. He was entirely too fond of teasing her. "You can skip the gloating and get to the part where you tell me what you heard. When I saw Roz and Jeanette on Friday afternoon, they certainly seemed to be friendly."

"I learned a few things during my interview with Jeanette's ex-husband, Bart." Nick paused and surveyed the shop. "I don't suppose we could sit down. If you're wanting to hear a story, we might as well be comfortable."

Kaylee nodded. "I can hear the front door from the consultation room. Do you want some coffee too?"

"That'd be great."

By the time Kaylee retrieved two mugs of coffee, Nick was settled on the consultation room love seat with Bear gazing up at him with doggy admiration. Kaylee laughed at his shameless quest for affection. She handed Nick his coffee. "Milk, two sugars. And I'm expecting a good story." She perched on her usual chair. Bear changed alliances then, trotting over to sit at Kaylee's ankles. She reached down to pet him.

Nick took a long sip of coffee. "Marlow very much blames Roz for a lot of the conflict in his marriage to Jeanette. He said

Roz stoked the flames whenever Jeanette got annoyed with him, and Jeanette finally figured that out. Apparently Jeanette and Roz weren't speaking when Jeanette left the island. Bart admitted he wasn't happy about her returning to visit Roz because he was worried Roz would change Jeanette's mind. He said he and Jeanette were planning to get back together."

"An interesting story, but I saw no sign of animosity on Friday," Kaylee said.

"Maybe they made up, or at least pretended to. You're putting a lot of weight on a brief encounter."

"Yes, but it's the only one I had, so it's all I really have to go on. And speaking of encounters, have you talked to Pop Ronson, by any chance?" Kaylee asked. "Apparently he and Roz don't get along."

"So he killed her friend and framed her for murder?" Nick shook his head. "I did talk to him. Pop and Roz compete for many of the same charters. And from my conversation with him, he seems to think Roz must be a smuggler or engaged in some other nefarious activity. According to him, nothing else could explain how she gets so many more fares than he does since she's surly all the time."

"What do you think of that?"

Nick snorted. "I think that most things Pop Ronson says should be taken with a grain of salt."

Kaylee had a sudden thought. "Did you happen to mention to him that Roz and Jeanette had been drinking tea?"

"No," Nick said, his surprise obvious. "Why would I?"

"I have no idea, but he knew about the tea, which made me wonder. Apparently there's a rumor spreading that Roz had been drinking alcohol the night Jeanette disappeared. So why would Pop Ronson, a man who seems to be full of negative ideas about Roz, be the one person who brings up the tea when I talk to him?"

"I have no idea, but I doubt it's quite as ominous as you make it sound. Roz probably told him." Nick drained the last of his coffee. "As much as I appreciate the coffee and the discussion, I need to go."

"Fine. But before you leave, did you learn anything interesting when you went out on Roz's boat today?"

"I learned again that I don't enjoy being out on the water this time of year." Nick grinned. "Though at least I kept myself together, unlike *some* deputies I could name. Still, I can't imagine being on that boat Friday night. The weather is much milder today, and the seas were rough enough to turn anyone's face green."

After Nick left, Kaylee rinsed out the mugs and returned to tidying up, though she'd only just finished restacking the handmade soaps when the door opened and Margaret Olber came in, a collection of shopping bags looped over one arm.

"It's wonderfully bracing out today." She walked right over to Kaylee, then gazed admiringly down at the soap. "Oh, these are lovely. Are they locally made?"

"They are," Kaylee answered. "My friend DeeDee Wilcox makes them with goat's milk and lavender. She owns Between the Lines." Kaylee gestured up Main Street toward her friend's mystery bookshop.

"I'll definitely take some," Margaret said, bringing a bar up near her nose for an appreciative sniff. "They'll make great gifts for people in my office. I've been buying things all over Turtle Cove today. I have to admit, though, that most of it was for myself."

"We do have a wide selection of shops in a small area," Kaylee agreed.

"And they're so quaint and charming," Margaret gushed.

"Are you going to be staying in Turtle Cove for a while?" Kaylee asked, wondering if the town's appeal had lured the woman into staying despite her friend's disappearance.

"I think so," Margaret answered. "It feels a little strange to be here without Jeanette, but I keep hoping she'll turn up. Besides, I so rarely get away from the office, and I've already taken the time off. I decided to use it. It's so beautiful and peaceful here."

Kaylee certainly couldn't argue with that. She loved Turtle Cove, even on its grayest, chilliest days.

Margaret leaned toward Kaylee and spoke in a near whisper, despite the fact that no one else was in the shop. "I heard you're a bit of a local Miss Marple. I wondered if you might let me help you investigate? It sounds so exciting, and I always thought it would be wonderful to find myself in the midst of a mystery, tracking down clues. I really want to help. Jeanette is my friend, and I've been a little worried about her depression lately."

Kaylee eased back a step and spoke in a normal tone, not wanting to get caught up in silly games. "I understand your interest, considering Jeanette is your friend, but the Orcas Island Sheriff's Department is handling the investigation. My only role has been to examine some plant evidence."

Margaret's excited expression faded into obvious disappointment. "Of course. I'm sorry if I offended you."

"Oh, I wasn't offended," Kaylee hurried to say. "Say, it's about time I closed for the day. Would you care to go next door to Death by Chocolate with me for a cup of hot chocolate? Jess makes the best." Kaylee certainly didn't need another cup of coffee on top of what she'd had with Nick, but she could go for some cocoa. And she didn't want Margaret to think she was being brushed off. After all, from the bags she carried, it appeared that she'd been supporting Turtle Cove businesses all day.

The other woman's face brightened again. "That sounds wonderful."

Kaylee slipped on her coat, then bent to pat an eager Bear, who clearly had interpreted the coat as proof they were about to go outside. "I'm sorry, pal, but no dogs next door. I'll be back soon, and we'll head home."

Bear wagged his tail furiously, his expression hopeful right up until Kaylee gently closed the door in his face and locked it.

"He's very good at making you feel guilty," Margaret said.

"He's a master," Kaylee agreed. "But I'll make it up to him with a treat and an outing later."

They walked to Death by Chocolate quickly, and the late afternoon breeze tried to muss their hair as much as possible in the short distance. Kaylee brushed a few strands from her eyes as she hauled open the door. She found the little shop buzzing with excitement.

Jessica turned a wide-eyed stare toward Kaylee. "Have you heard the news?"

"Apparently not," Kaylee said, surveying the people in the room, all mirroring Jessica's expression of shock. "What happened?"

"They found Jeanette Colson," Jessica said breathlessly. "Her body washed up on the shoreline. She's dead."

8

Kaylee's head reeled at what she'd heard, and she realized that she'd truly never believed Jeanette was dead. Her shock must have shown on her face because she felt a hand on her arm.

"Are you all right?" Margaret asked. "You're white as a sheet."

"She's right, Kaylee." Jessica walked around the counter and helped Margaret lead Kaylee to the closest chair.

"I guess I thought Jeanette was playing some kind of trick," Kaylee said.

Margaret sank into a chair across the small table from Kaylee. "A trick?"

Kaylee shrugged. "To use Roz's boat for something . . . nefarious, I guess. I hadn't thought it through."

Margaret nodded solemnly. "Me either. I kept expecting Jeanette to simply show up."

"Well, I suppose she did. Just not the way anyone wanted her to." This came from a woman Kaylee didn't recognize who stood near the bakery's glass display case, which was filled with enticing chocolate treats. The juxtaposition of the callous comment and the beautiful desserts made Kaylee's stomach roll.

"Let me get you some hot chocolate," Jessica suggested. "The sugar will help with the shock."

Kaylee managed to nod, then focused on taking long slow breaths and waiting for the odd sensation to pass. Margaret reached across the table to pat her arm again. "I wonder if Jeanette simply didn't want Roz to see her jump into the water."

"Jump into the water?" Kaylee blinked at the other woman. *Who would jump into that rough water in the middle of a February* night? The cold would kill you in minutes. Unless that was the whole point. "You think it was suicide," she said flatly.

Margaret turned her palms up. "I can't be sure, of course, but Jeanette has been depressed on and off for at least the last year. I had so hoped this trip would help improve her mood."

"She appeared very happy when I saw her Friday afternoon." Kaylee felt as if that line was becoming her refrain.

"She could do that." Margaret shrugged. "At work she'd seem perfectly normal, and then I'd walk into the restroom and hear her crying in one of the stalls. I think she was a very troubled woman."

"But she'd been with Roz for days," Kaylee said. "Surely Roz would have noticed if Jeanette was depressed."

"You can never tell what's going on inside a person. Some people are good at hiding, I guess."

Jessica arrived and handed Kaylee a cup of hot chocolate. She also gave one to Margaret, then offered her hand. "I'm Jessica Roberts. This is my shop."

Margaret gave her a small smile. "Margaret Olber."

"Are you okay, Kaylee?" Jessica asked as she sat in the third seat at the table.

Kaylee felt her cheeks warm at all the attention to her unexpected reaction. "I'm fine," she said. "Honestly, I only met Jeanette the one time, but the news was such a shock."

Jessica folded her hands and rested them on the table. "I get it. She and Roz were so funny when they were in here. They reminded me of a new version of *The Odd Couple*—two friends who couldn't be more different and contrary."

"Margaret thinks it might have been suicide," Kaylee said, lowering her voice so it wouldn't be overheard by the people glancing at them curiously from the front counter.

"We worked together. I knew her fairly well." Margaret

issued a dry, mirthless laugh. "Or so I thought. Honestly, how well can we know anyone?"

"I'd think her ex-husband would know her," Kaylee said. "He says that he and Jeanette were getting back together, but he didn't mention any depression."

"And that's interesting," Margaret said, "considering she never mentioned getting back together with her ex. The only things I ever heard her say about him were negative. Very negative."

"Have you shared that with the police?" Kaylee asked.

Margaret shook her head. "It didn't come up."

"You might want to tell them."

Margaret's lips curled into something that didn't quite qualify as a smile. "Perhaps I will."

At the sound of the front door's bell jingling, Jessica glanced up. "I'd better get back to the register," she said. "Nice to meet you, Margaret."

After Jessica returned to her work, Margaret gulped down her chocolate quickly and excused herself. "I wanted to go pick up some snacks for my room before returning to the inn. It was good to see you, Kaylee."

Kaylee offered something equally innocuous and watched the woman head out of the shop. Margaret Olber seemed strange, and Kaylee wasn't sure what to make of her. But she wasn't going to play detective with the woman. She had more than enough mysteries on her plate right now.

The recently arrived customers browsing at the sweets display made and paid for their choices before Kaylee finished with her hot chocolate, so Jessica came back over to sit with her. "All better?"

"The curative power of hot chocolate has done its wonders again," Kaylee assured her. "What did you make of Margaret?"

"She's an odd duck, don't you think? And I'm still not

convinced Jeanette was depressed, no matter what she says."

"I do agree that you can't always tell what's going on with someone," Kaylee said tentatively. "And we didn't chat with Jeanette very long."

"True, but I'm an excellent judge of character." Then Jessica's expression darkened and she raised a finger. "Though Oliver is an even better one. And he did drop a leaf after Jeanette was in here on Friday. Remember? Maybe he could tell something was wrong with her."

Kaylee resisted the urge to chuckle. "Wouldn't he have dropped it *while* she was in here?"

"It might be hard work to drop a leaf that way," Jessica said. Then she leaned forward. "So what are you going to do next?"

"Next?"

"In the investigation. Don't pretend you're not going to do anything. You're wearing your interrogation face. Who are you off to question?"

"I'm off to collect Bear," Kaylee said. "And he's very resistant to questioning."

"So you're not going to tell me?" Jessica pouted.

Kaylee relented. "I did think I might drop by the inn and chat with Jeanette's ex if he's up for it. He was friendly enough when I met him at the ferry."

"He could be in a state now." Jessica's expression was sympathetic. "He was probably hoping for a happy ending. Especially if he thought they were getting back together." She raised an eyebrow at Kaylee. "Make sure you pass along what you find out. Oliver is still worried. I can tell."

"I can't be sure that I'll find out anything, but I'll keep you posted for Oliver's peace of mind—or leaf." Kaylee stood. "For now, I'm off to collect my best guy."

"Give Bear a hug from me."

After she did a few last-minute chores at the flower shop, Kaylee snapped a leash on Bear and headed for the car. The Northern Lights Inn was a walkable distance during most of the year, but despite the slightly warmer day, Kaylee wasn't interested in trying to walk that far without freezing, especially not since night still came distressingly early.

The owner of the Northern Lights didn't restrict pets, so she carried Bear in with her. As soon as she came through the door, the little dog gave a yip of excitement, and Kaylee was surprised to see a cat dart behind a potted plant.

She walked over to the check-in desk and addressed the young woman standing behind the counter. "Did one of the guests' cats slip downstairs?"

"No, that's Lucky," the employee said. The desk agent was new, or at least new to Kaylee, and she wore a name badge that said her name was Stella. "She was left behind by one of the guests—can you imagine? She's the inn mascot for the winter. The boss says we'll have to find her a home before our big spring-cleaning. She doesn't want to risk Lucky triggering allergies."

"I thought you accepted pet guests," Kaylee said.

"We do," Stella agreed. "But we do have some pet-free rooms, which are hard to keep clean of allergens when there's a cat running around the building. Especially one as curious about everything as Lucky. She keeps sneaking into rooms when the maids clean."

"Well, you know what they say about cats and curiosity."

Stella offered a lopsided smile. "I hope that's not the case for poor Lucky. She's a sweetie. Since we aren't exactly bustling this month, we can be more relaxed." She leaned closer and dropped her voice. "We actually have a lot more guests right now than we expected."

"Really?" Bear was wriggling in her arms so Kaylee set him

down, shaking a finger near his nose. "Behave. Don't chase the cat."

Bear licked the end of her finger, totally unimpressed by her effort to sound stern. However, although he stood focused on the plant where the cat hid, he didn't tug the leash to get closer to Lucky.

When Kaylee straightened again, the young woman picked up the conversation immediately. "We have four rooms rented, though one of them belongs to the lady who died. The only people going in and out of that one are the deputies."

Kaylee perked up at that. She'd wondered where Jeanette had stayed. "I don't suppose I could see inside Jeanette's room?"

"No way." Stella's appalled tone matched her wide eyes. "It would be my job if I agreed to that."

"Sorry," Kaylee said conciliatorily, then she offered her hand. "By the way, I'm Kaylee Bleu. I own The Flower Patch."

"My mom loves that place." The young woman shook Kaylee's hand. "I'm Stella Dunmore. Stella means star. My dad is way into stars."

"That's a nice hobby."

"Except when he drags you out in the cold to squint through a telescope." Stella studied Kaylee. "I've heard about you. You're some kind of detective."

"Hardly," Kaylee said. "I'm a forensic botanist. I do help the sheriff's department sometimes."

"Forensic?" Stella's face brightened with excitement. "Like on TV? The science people who solve crimes? That's so cool."

Kaylee decided not to correct Stella's assumption about the amount she was involved in crime solving. "I don't suppose that changes your mind about showing me Jeanette's room?"

Stella plucked at her glossy lower lip while she considered it. "I'd better not. Maybe if you came back with a deputy?"

Kaylee seriously doubted she could get any of the deputies to go along with that, although it was possible if she could convince Nick that she needed to search the room for traces of valerian root. "I'll consider that."

Stella leaned forward, arms on the counter. "Have you heard the rumor?"

"Rumor?" Kaylee echoed.

"That Roz Corzo and the dead woman went out in that storm the other night and got blackout drunk," Stella said, her voice squeaky with the scandal of it. "And then that woman fell overboard. She probably drowned. That's going to be bad for Roz's business."

"Actually no alcohol was involved," Kaylee said firmly.

Stella grew even more excited, likely at the prospect of getting a scoop from Kaylee. "Do you have the whole story?"

"I wouldn't be much of a forensic botanist if I revealed details of an investigation," Kaylee said, hoping she sounded properly stern and official.

Stella gave Kaylee a sly nod. "Of course. Mum's the word." Then she leaned forward even farther. "So why are you here?"

"I'm here to speak with Bart Marlow."

"Oh. He's in his room. Second floor, first door to the left of the stairs."

"Thanks, Stella. I appreciate your help."

Stella beamed at her, and Kaylee led Bear upstairs. She found the door easily enough and tapped on it. Bart opened the door, and Kaylee immediately noticed the man's red, swollen eyes.

He squinted at her as if it took some effort to place her. "Miss Bleu," he said finally in a slightly hoarse voice. "How can I help you?"

"I'm so sorry to intrude at this horrible time," Kaylee said, suddenly awash with guilt at bothering this man when he was clearly grieving. "I wanted to ask you something, but . . ."

He opened the door wider. "No, that's all right. Please, come in. I would welcome the company and the distraction. This isn't a good time for me to be alone with my thoughts."

The room was tidy and filled with charming touches, including the handmade quilt on the double bed and the rocking chair near the window where guests could sit and gaze toward the bay during daylight hours. But in one corner, a small suitcase rested against a box fan and several furnace filters.

"Were those Jeanette's?" Kaylee asked, pointing.

"Yes, the inn brought them to me. Technically Lyle is Jeanette's next of kin, but he told them to throw everything away so they thought I might want it."

"Do those filters fit your furnace?"

He shook his head. "I imagine they're for a dehydrator."

"Excuse me?"

"Years ago, Jeanette saw some cooking show where a guy made a dehydrator from a box fan and furnace filters. She said it was much better for drying herbs than the one I bought her." He sighed. "Sometimes it felt as if there was always something better than whatever I did."

"Do you mind if I examine the filters?" Kaylee asked. When he agreed, she held each filter under the light. She saw threadlike roots on all of them. She carefully extracted a bit of root and slipped it into an envelope from her purse.

"Is that important?" Bart asked.

"It answers a question I had," she said, pocketing the envelope. "And speaking of questions, I had heard something odd, and I thought you might be able to confirm it for me."

"Sure, come sit."

The man waved Kaylee toward the rocker. She sat down, and Bear settled near her feet.

Bart gazed sadly at the dog. "I've often thought I should get a pet," he said. "But I'm away from home a lot. Still, it would be pleasant to have a little dog."

Seeing the opportunity to find out whether he had a house, Kaylee pressed on. "It can be hard to keep a dog in an apartment. I've been there myself."

"That wouldn't be a problem. I have a house," he said. "But even then, dogs don't adjust well to being alone so much."

"Bear hates when I leave him alone for too long," Kaylee agreed, thinking that she had one question answered. When Jeanette told Smith she would soon have room to grow plants, she might have been talking about reuniting with Bart.

Bart's expression remained almost blank as Kaylee thought through what she'd learned, but he finally asked, "What did you want to know, Miss Bleu?"

Kaylee took a breath before broaching the subject of Jeanette's supposed depression. "A coworker of Jeanette's said that she'd seen Jeanette crying in the restroom at work. She thought Jeanette was depressed."

Bart shook his head slowly. "No. She wasn't. She was very happy at the way our relationship was going. We were making plans. She was full of hope for our future. I'm sure of that."

"She certainly seemed happy when I talked to her on Friday," Kaylee said.

Bart watched her intently. "I'm glad." A silent pause stretched between them before he spoke again, his voice soft with the weight of emotion. "I should have come with her. She said it would be better if she came alone so she could patch things up with Roz. But if I'd come over, she might . . ." His voice choked and he stopped talking. He leaned forward and held his head in his hands.

"You couldn't force her," Kaylee said consolingly. "And I can see why she'd want to mend fences with Roz. She'd clearly mended a big one with you."

Bart glanced up and wiped his eyes with the edge of his hands. "She loved Roz like a sister at one time. She told me that she felt she needed Roz's blessing for us or something. Before we officially got back together."

Kaylee thought that sounded strange. If Jeanette hadn't seen Roz in years, why would Roz's opinion matter? "What did you think about that?"

He shrugged. "I thought it was silly, but I didn't say so. I couldn't picture Roz ever agreeing that us getting back together was a good idea. I figured it just was something Jeanette had to get out of her system. Now I think maybe she needed that blessing more than I ever imagined. Maybe when she didn't get it, it drove her to drastic measures."

"What do you mean?"

"One of the deputies said they thought maybe Jeanette drowned herself," Bart explained. "I guess they talked to that coworker as well. I'll tell you right now, though, that she wasn't depressed before she came here. *If* she killed herself, it must have had something to do with Roz. Roz could be such a bull in a china shop, especially with people's feelings. Maybe she crushed Jeanette's hopes somehow."

"You really think that?"

"It's a possibility anyway. Honestly, I never understood Jeanette's fondness for that abrasive woman." Bart sighed and his shoulders slumped. "At first, I was sure it was Roz who killed her. I guess a lot of the old resentment flooded back when I heard Jeanette had disappeared. And I didn't want to consider anything else. I was terrified that Jeanette had left me again. I needed to blame someone, so I didn't consider that possibility too closely."

"You thought Jeanette might have left you?"

"She'd done it before, and I hadn't seen it coming then either.

Jeanette was a complicated woman, but I loved her."

Kaylee considered her next question. She was on delicate ground. The man seemed eager to open up, but that could go bad quickly if she said the wrong thing. "What do you think drove you two apart the first time?"

"Truly? I think it was mistrust." Again he hunched over, appearing for all the world like a man in terrible pain.

"Mistrust? On whose part?"

"I thought Jeanette spent too much time with another man, an herbalist named Smith Hooper. She was always out at his place. He was older and I thought he was crazy, but Jeanette had always been one for odd obsessions. I worried that their relationship might be about more than plants and tea. Then when Jeanette knew I disapproved, she started lying and saying she was with Roz instead. What was I supposed to think?"

Kaylee couldn't imagine Jeanette having romantic inclinations toward the herbalist, but that seemed to be exactly what Bart had thought. "That must have been hard."

Bart fidgeted a little, then continued. "I may have made some wild assumptions back then, but now I think Hooper was more of a father figure. At the time, though, I felt rejected. Jeanette had this sudden huge passion for herbalism, and I was shut out from that."

Kaylee could tell by Bart's long pauses and restless movements that he was growing tired of the conversation. Did she dare press on? She decided to ask one more question. "How did Jeanette get along with her family? With her brother?"

Bart's expression darkened and Kaylee almost expected him to yell at her. "I can't stand that guy, and he hated Jeanette. I'm not fooled by this sudden display of concern for her. He was jealous of her. If she'd died on the mainland, Lyle would have been my prime suspect."

"He was jealous of Jeanette?"

Bart nodded. "Their parents doted on Jeanette, probably more than was healthy, if I'm being honest. She was accomplished and charming, and Lyle was a dim-witted, sullen lump. He's an unsuccessful fisherman who lives on a boat he's in danger of losing to the bank. He has no friends to speak of. He blamed Jeanette for the way his parents treated him, but I think he should have considered himself and the role he played in the things he's experienced."

"So why would he act so concerned about Jeanette's disappearance?" Kaylee asked.

"Probably guilt after hating her all his life."

Bart rubbed his hands over his pants, clearly about to stand, and Kaylee suspected she was about to be bid good night. She quickly injected another question. "How good was Jeanette with boats? If Roz was incapacitated, could she have handled the boat and gotten them safely to the wharf?"

"Oh sure," he said as he stood. "She and I both had had years of experience. We had a boat together when we lived here on Orcas." He squinted toward the window, his expression sad. "Selling the boat and dividing the profits between us during the divorce was what finally made the whole thing real. And painful. It took me years to save up enough for another boat. My new one isn't half as nice."

Kaylee realized Bart was ready to be rid of her and stood. "Thank you so much for giving me your time. I appreciate it."

"No problem," he said. "When the sheriff's deputy came by with the news about Jeanette's . . ." He stopped and breathed deeply a few times. "About her passing, I had a lot to think about. It was actually helpful to process some of it with someone. But I'm exhausted now."

"Of course," Kaylee said. "And I'm deeply sorry for your loss."

"Thank you." He walked her and Bear the few paces to the door and let them out.

When the door closed behind her, Kaylee stood pondering what Bart had told her. The fact that he had suspected there was more to Jeanette and Mr. Hooper's relationship than met the eye deserved consideration. Had more happened during Jeanette's visit to the herbalist than Mr. Hooper had let on? Did he hold a grudge against her for something else?

If so, he wouldn't be the only one, nor the one most likely to do her harm on the water. Jeanette's brother, Lyle, apparently hated her, and he had a boat, so he could have gone out to Roz's boat that night, pushed her overboard, and then returned to the mainland. Of course, Pop Ronson had a boat as well, and he hated Roz. She couldn't imagine why he'd hurt Jeanette, though—unless it had been a case of mistaken identity.

But none of those theories synced up with the fact that Jeanette had stolen valerian root from Mr. Hooper, ostensibly dried it, and put it into the tea she'd served her friend—the friend captaining the boat they were taking out at night on tumultuous waters. With that in mind, Jeanette must have had something to do with her own death—but why?

"The problem with this situation," Kaylee murmured to Bear. "Is that we have entirely too many motives and not enough clues."

"I knew it!" shouted a voice behind her.

9

Kaylee jumped, and Bear yipped with surprise. She spun to discover Margaret standing at the top of the stairs with her hands on her hips.

"I *knew* you were investigating," Margaret continued, her voice somewhere between accusatory and excited.

"This isn't a game," Kaylee said, keeping her voice calm and quiet in the hopes Margaret would emulate her. She didn't want Bart to hear them.

The other woman's triumphant stance vanished. "Let me help," she said beseechingly. "Jeanette was my friend. You only met her once. I could be helpful in judging what you've learned."

"The sheriff's department is investigating," Kaylee said. "I'm going home. I've had a long day, and I need to walk Bear and get some supper."

"I wish you'd let me help," Margaret muttered in a sulky tone that would have better suited a teenager than a woman in her forties.

"If you can share anything helpful, you should do so with the sheriff's department. They do excellent work."

Margaret narrowed her eyes, but it was clear she'd given up begging. "Fine. I'll do that."

Suddenly Bear lunged against the leash, releasing a few sharp barks as he strained against Kaylee's hold.

"Bear, what's going on with you?" Kaylee searched the landing for what had excited the little dog, and she spotted Lucky the cat rushing up the stairs.

The cat ignored Bear completely and headed straight for

Margaret's purse, an oversize leather bag on a long strap. The cat leaped for the purse, but Margaret pulled it up and clutched it to her chest just in time.

"Go away!" Margaret said, her voice high with alarm. "Make it go away!"

Lucky tried to climb the front of Margaret's pants, making the woman yelp. Kaylee quickly went to help, making a grab for the clawing cat while Bear yipped and danced at her feet.

"Cut it out, Lucky!" Kaylee caught hold of the cat and was grateful not to get scratched in the process. Lucky squirmed desperately, never taking her eyes off Margaret's purse. "Do you have food in your purse?" Kaylee asked. "Fish maybe?"

"My to-go box isn't an open invitation to be attacked." Margaret backed away. "That animal shouldn't be allowed to run around loose. It's dangerous." She groped behind her for the handle to her door without taking her eyes off the cat. Then she darted inside and slammed the door.

The moment the door was closed, the cat wiggled free from Kaylee's grip and rushed over to meow at the door. Kaylee sighed. *You're not going to make it to spring at this rate, Lucky.*

Bear strained at the end of the leash to reach Lucky, wagging his tail. The cat spun to face him. Kaylee held her breath, hoping Bear wasn't about to catch a face full of claws. Fortunately, Lucky sniffed noses with Bear.

Kaylee scooped up Lucky again. The cat wriggled, then seemed to change focus and tried to shove her head into Kaylee's coat pocket.

"You're a handful," Kaylee said, shifting the cat in her arms and holding her firmly as she headed downstairs with Bear in tow on his leash. She carried the cat over to Stella. "Lucky has developed an obsession with Margaret Olber's handbag. Apparently Margaret brought home a to-go box. I suspect she must have had fish for dinner." She set the cat on the desk. "You might want to keep her away from Margaret for a while until she calms down."

"Oh dear," Stella said. "How mad is she?"

Kaylee grimaced. "Lucky tried to climb the front of her pants and I think she might have gotten some scratches from that. So she's not exactly happy."

Stella raised a hand to her cheek as the cat sprawled on the counter and began washing her face as if she didn't have a care in the world. "I'll call the boss. This could be terrible."

Kaylee peered at the cat. Lucky was certainly acting normally now. "Maybe Lucky isn't getting enough dinner," Kaylee suggested. Then she had a thought. "You might want to take her to a vet. If she's pregnant, she might be hungry."

"Pregnant!" Stella shook her head. "The boss won't appreciate that a bit."

Kaylee patted Lucky, who bumped her head against Kaylee's hand, purring loudly. "At any rate, you might give her bigger dinners. It might take her mind off anyone bringing food upstairs."

"I'll do that now." Stella scooped up Lucky and carried her off.

After a quick walk around the parking lot with Bear, Kaylee headed for home.

"I think we should have a chat with Nick," Kaylee told Bear as they drove. "I want to see if he's checked on Bart and Lyle's boats yet."

Bear offered a sleepy grumble that sounded like disagreement.

"You're right," Kaylee said. "Both men owning boats doesn't explain why Jeanette wanted to incapacitate Roz, and it's clear that she did. She probably kept Roz up late Thursday night for the sole purpose of being sure the valerian would knock her out on Friday."

The drive home reminded Kaylee of how rarely she'd seen

true darkness when she lived in Seattle. On Orcas Island, the streetlights didn't extend far from town, so by the time Kaylee neared Wildflower Cottage, her headlights seemed to be cutting holes in the inky night. Fortunately, the exterior light she'd set on a timer was illuminated to greet her. In the darkness, however, the bulb did little more than mark the door's location.

Once parked, she and Bear climbed out of the car. The night was still and cold, but Kaylee could hear the sound of waves breaking against rocks in the distance. The weather was surprisingly clear, and she marveled at the stars that glittered across the sky, a gift in the darkness. "I don't think I could ever return to Seattle. I'd miss this place too much," she told Bear. After enjoying the peace a while longer, she asked, "Do you want to walk a little before we go in?"

The little dog hustled off across the lawn. Kaylee started after him, only to see Bear freeze, standing stiffly and staring out into the darkness.

"What's wrong?" she asked.

Bear's response was to launch into a flurry of barks and growls. Kaylee ran to him and stared hard into the darkness, as if effort alone could improve her night vision. She didn't see anything, and a chill that had nothing to do with the night air crept up her spine. "Is anyone there?" she called out.

She received no answer, and eventually Bear quieted, though he continued to glare into the night, growls rumbling in his chest. "I think we'd better go inside, Bear," she said. She gathered up the reluctant dog and hurried into the house, locking the door again once they were inside.

Bear rushed to the window that faced the area of the yard he'd been watching and hopped up on an ottoman so he could see out.

"Why don't you come and eat?" Kaylee asked, hoping that the mention of food would draw him away from the window.

It didn't.

In fact, Bear maintained a vigil at the window, growling occasionally for at least half an hour before finally settling down and going to his food bowl.

While Bear ate, Kaylee walked over to peer out the window, but she couldn't see a thing. "It was probably a raccoon," she said quietly, then decided not to say anything else that evening. Somehow her voice in the still house didn't help her nerves at all.

After eating her own dinner, Kaylee settled down with a book and finally managed to relax enough to stop reading the same page over and over. She kept an eye on Bear, but he never went to the window again. In fact, he flopped down at her feet and promptly fell asleep. *I'm glad you can relax*, she thought drily, knowing full well that, for her, drifting off to sleep that night wouldn't be so easy.

On Thursday morning, Kaylee poured herself a cup of strong coffee, hoping for a restorative effect to overcome the poor sleep of the night before. She'd awakened more than once and checked all the locks.

"It's your fault," she told Bear as he cheerfully gobbled down his breakfast. "You're the one who tried to convince me that we had Bigfoot in the backyard."

Bear gazed up at her and wagged his tail, then he whipped around and raced for the door, barking.

"Now what?" she groaned. She followed Bear to the door and peered through the window but didn't see anything. At her feet, Bear continued to wag his tail furiously. That's when Kaylee recognized the rumble of an approaching vehicle.

She walked outside as a shiny, black Ford pickup made its way up the drive. Kaylee felt a rush of joy at the sight of it. "Reese!" she called out as the driver's side door swung open. "When did you get home?"

"Yesterday," he said as he climbed out of the truck carrying a small cardboard box. "I would have come by the shop to say hi, but I had a pile of mail and messages to deal with. I think everything in Turtle Cove broke while I was gone." The smile he aimed at her was so warm it seemed to drive away every bit of the February chill buffeting Kaylee.

"We like you to feel needed," Kaylee said, keeping her tone light and friendly. She hadn't realized how much she'd missed Reese during the stress of the last few days. There was something comforting about having him around. "Do you want to come in for some coffee? It's too cold out here to chat."

"That sounds fantastic." When he caught up to Kaylee, he handed over the box. "From my mom. They were waiting at the post office when I got home. She sent them for you."

Kaylee studied the unopened box curiously, wondering what Camila Holt, whom she'd never met, might have sent her all the way from California. "What is it?"

"Flower bulbs," he answered as he followed her into the house. "Mom divided up some of her irises this year. She thought you might be interested in a few as she has some unusual colors. There's a note inside that will make a lot more sense of it than I can."

"How thoughtful of her. I'm sure I'll love them." Kaylee waved Reese toward the kitchen table and poured him a mug of coffee. She added a splash of milk but no sugar and handed it to him.

"Exactly the way I like it," he said, giving her that smile that made her insides flutter a little. Kaylee quickly tamped down such silliness. *Goodness, wouldn't Mary have a field day teasing me about that?*

"Did your talk go well?" she asked.

He nodded. "Better than things have gone around here apparently. I was sorry to hear about Roz's friend. I didn't get the woman's name, but I heard about her death."

"Jeanette Colson, maybe Jeanette Marlow when she lived here. Ring any bells?"

Reese shook his head. "If I ever met her, I don't remember her. We get folks moving on and off the island all the time. Local gossip says she might have killed herself."

"That's one version of the rumor," Kaylee said. "Another common belief is that Roz killed her."

Reese drew back, clearly surprised. "That's ridiculous. Roz isn't exactly cuddly, but she's not going to kill her friends."

"As you can imagine, Roz is pretty upset," Kaylee said. "She insisted I clear her name."

"And I'm sure you told her no." Reese grinned at her over his mug. He knew full well that Kaylee would never say no to someone who needed help—especially not someone as stubborn as Roz.

Kaylee sighed and settled into the chair across from him. "I don't think I've gotten very far, unfortunately."

"As long as you're staying safe."

"I haven't gotten into any trouble, don't worry." Kaylee hesitated. "Well, last night was a little weird, but I don't think it was related."

Reese's gaze sharpened. "Last night? What happened?"

Kaylee explained about Bear's odd behavior. "Once he calmed down, he never went back to the window. I think it must have been a raccoon or something."

"Maybe." Reese set his mug on the table. "Can you show

me where you were and whatever you think Bear seemed to be interested in?"

"If you want." Kaylee slipped into her heavy coat and led Bear and Reese outside. She paused at the spot where she'd stood the previous evening. In the clear light of morning, all her nerves from the night before seemed silly, and she was embarrassed that she'd brought it up at all. "Bear and I were here." She pointed. "He was all worked up about something in that direction. I'm sure it was only local wildlife."

"You're probably right." Reese headed across the yard and Kaylee followed. Bear trotted along beside her, clearly unconcerned about anything.

Kaylee felt increasingly foolish, her face growing hot despite the weather. "I'm sure it's nothing, Reese. Honestly, I hate to have you out in the cold over something so silly."

Reese kept walking, though he called over his shoulder, "I have faith in Bear. If he thought there was something worth growling at, I want to know what he saw." Then Reese stopped suddenly. "Kaylee, come here."

She hurried over and examined the spot that Reese was indicating. Near the corner of the property, the ground was especially soft from the recent rain. And deep in the soft soil, she could see a clear footprint. Someone had been out in her yard. *But who? And why?*

10

Though Kaylee and Bear were late getting to the shop, no one hovered outside waiting to buy emergency flowers, not that she'd expected anyone. Still, she decided to skip sneaking over to Death by Chocolate for coffee. She could make her own, of course, though she never quite managed to replicate the great coffee Mary prepared for them.

She checked on the arrangements already waiting in the coolers and refreshed one that had some wilted petals. Bear trotted along behind her as she completed the morning tasks. Each time she stopped to accomplish something, Bear would sit, his long nose pointed up at her like an arrow, as if ready in case she needed him for anything. *Or in case a treat should happen to fall from the sky.*

When the front door opened and a pair of older women came in, Bear trotted over to welcome them, his tail wagging. "Well," the taller woman said, "aren't you a handsome little guy with your dapper yellow bow tie?"

Bear wriggled with joy. He definitely knew a compliment when he heard one.

"We drove over from Eastsound," the second woman told Kaylee. "We heard you had the most adorable arrangements and handmade soap. We wanted to get some to take to the senior center. This time of year, it can be hard to keep everyone's spirits up."

"What a kind idea," Kaylee said as she led the women to the cooler that held the collection of small ready-to-buy arrangements. They both cooed over the color choices and cute accessories. They picked out several and then bought Kaylee's entire stock of soap for the seniors to enjoy.

"I can hardly wait to get to the senior center and see those faces light up," the shorter woman said, beaming at Kaylee. "We'll definitely be back."

After thanking them, Kaylee watched the two ladies chatting happily as they left, and she thought how nice it was to see people concerned about others. It was easy to simply huddle and wish for a quick spring, but those women were doing something to bring sunshine even in the gloom.

"You know, Bear," Kaylee said, "maybe we should take some flowers to that senior center sometime. You'd love to make some new friends there, wouldn't you?"

Bear yipped in agreement as Kaylee picked up the soap display and slipped it behind the counter. She didn't want customers to come in and wonder at the empty racks.

"I think we might need to walk over to Between the Lines," Kaylee said. "It's possible DeeDee has some soap at the store. And I want to check on a book I ordered."

Kaylee frowned when he didn't respond to the mention of a walk, then turned as she heard the bell jingle over the front door. The little dog bounded over to greet Nick, who had just walked in. He bent to pat Bear, but the look he gave Kaylee was reproving.

"I ran into Reese buying coffee next door," Nick said. "I suspect he'll be along. He wasn't happy that you hadn't called me about an intruder at your house."

"Intruder is a stretch," Kaylee said. "I'm sure it's nothing. Probably someone out for a walk."

Nick stood. "In February? It hasn't exactly been walking weather, especially late at night."

"It wasn't that late. Besides, some people aren't deterred by the weather when it comes to exercise." When the deputy's expression remained dubious, she sighed. "I'm not worried, Nick. No one had been in the cottage. I'm careful about locking up. And Bear was totally fine after he calmed down."

"And I have a lot of respect for Bear's discernment, but I still think you should have called me."

"At the time, I thought it was probably a raccoon," Kaylee said. "Or maybe a deer. And if you'd discovered it was an animal, I would have felt like an idiot."

"Being careful is never foolish. I'd rather check on your place and find there's nothing to be concerned about than not check and have something happen."

"If you want to go out and stare at the footprint Reese found, be my guest," Kaylee said. "But I refuse to fret about it. However, since you're here, I am curious about something. What was Jeanette's time of death?"

Nick huffed. "The time of death was impossible to pinpoint accurately because of the icy water. It could have been almost anytime during the night she disappeared or even early the next morning. We're still waiting on the full report from a lab on the mainland."

"It's slow coming."

"Right now, we can't rule out accident or suicide, and both of those push the case down the priority list. The lab on the mainland is busy, but we should get the report soon."

"Both Bart and Lyle have boats. Do they have alibis for the night of Jeanette's disappearance?"

Nick eyed her in surprise. "You don't think their ferry trip was the first time they'd come over recently?"

"Maybe not. Though I couldn't exactly see them working together. They clearly don't get along."

"Clearly." Nick leaned on the counter, his gaze on Bear. The little dog was staring pointedly at the door. "Neither has a solid alibi for the night she disappeared, though if she didn't die until morning, it might have been tight for either of them to get over here, murder her, then get to the mainland in time to ride the ferry over on Monday."

"What were they doing?"

"Lyle was on his boat. The bank foreclosed on his house, and he has basically been living on the fishing boat ever since. He was very cagey about whether he took the boat out at all on that night. I can't tell if it's because he was doing something to Jeanette or maybe doing something else of dubious legality."

"For example?"

"Fishing outside of acceptable areas," Nick said. "Or maybe even smuggling. I hate to speculate wildly, but I don't like the guy and wouldn't put a lot past him."

"How about Bart?" Kaylee asked, though she felt a little guilty about that. Bart had certainly seemed torn up about Jeanette's death.

"He says he was home alone, missing Jeanette and eagerly anticipating her return," Nick said. "I have some contacts on the mainland checking into both men."

"Well, I have a little news myself," Kaylee said. "You remember the box fan and the furnace filters? They were for a homemade dehydrator. The inn gave Jeanette's things to Bart, and I saw them. He's the one who told me she rigged a dryer made from filters and a box fan. And I found root strands caught in a filter. I took a sample, but I haven't had a chance to examine it under a microscope yet. Still, I'm fairly sure from a visual inspection that it's valerian root."

"Apparently I'll have to collect those filters," Nick said. "They've become evidence after all."

The jingle of the bell over the door heralded Reese's entrance. He carried two cups of coffee from Death by Chocolate. "I brought you a thank-you coffee, Kaylee."

"Not that I'm complaining, but I don't know what you're thanking me for," Kaylee said, accepting one of the cups. "You brought me new flower bulbs and then walked around in the cold to check for intruders."

"True," Reese said. "But you did give me my first coffee of the day, and it was much appreciated."

Nick laughed, and both Kaylee and Reese gawked at him. He grinned at them both. "Like Reese needed an excuse to want to come in here."

Kaylee felt her face warm at Nick's teasing. She snuck a glance at Reese but couldn't quite interpret the expression on his face. Was he embarrassed by Nick's joking too?

"You have a point," Reese said finally. "I am always glad to visit Kaylee and Bear." Then his gaze swept the shop. "And Mary too. Where's she hiding?"

"She has the day off," Kaylee said, glad that the awkward moment had passed.

"Good for her," Reese said. Then he gave Kaylee a severe expression not unlike the one Nick had worn when he'd come in. "And I have a bone to pick with you. Nick said you didn't call him after we found that footprint."

"I didn't exactly have time. I had to open the shop, and then I had customers, and then Nick showed up anyway because *someone* tattled on me," Kaylee protested. "Honestly, it was probably somebody taking a walk. You two have got to stop making me paranoid."

"We don't want you to be paranoid," Nick said.

"We want you to be careful," Reese finished.

Kaylee held up both hands. "Fine. I'll be careful. I'll take Bear with me everywhere I go. I can't be much safer than that." Bear yipped at his name.

"That should do it," Nick said drily. "Your great protector."

Before Kaylee could say anything else, the door opened, and Bear backed up close to Reese's leg and growled. "What's wrong, buddy?" Reese asked as he bent to scoop up the dog.

Lyle Colson stormed through the door and scowled at all of them before stabbing a finger toward Nick. "I saw you through the window, laughing it up with your buddies. Have you found out who killed my sister yet, or are you even bothering to investigate?"

Nick continued to lean on the counter and now he crossed his arms, regarding the angry man calmly. "We haven't confirmed that *anyone* killed your sister, but I promise that we are pursuing every lead."

"Of course someone killed her, and it's clear as day who did it! Arrest that Corzo woman!" Lyle roared, sending Bear into a frenzy.

Reese walked around the angry man to stand next to Kaylee. Lyle wasn't paying Kaylee any attention, but it was clear Reese intended to be in place in case that changed. She appreciated the gesture.

"You need to calm down," Nick warned.

"A murderer is wandering around loose while my sister is dead, and you have a problem with my attitude?" Lyle bellowed.

"Not only do I have a problem with it," Nick said, "I'm willing to take you in for creating a disturbance in Ms. Bleu's place of business."

Lyle took a few deep breaths, clearly struggling for control. Finally, he spoke in a quieter voice, though Kaylee saw that he still stood rigidly with both fists clenched. "Bart told me that Roz and Jeanette had a lot of bad blood from the days Jeanette lived here. Who else on this island could have had reason to hurt my sister?"

With Lyle clearly calming down, Reese set Bear on the

floor behind the counter, though he never took his gaze from the angry man.

"We still don't know that your sister's death was anything more than an accident," Nick said, matching the other man's calmer tone. "If we find out that someone did hurt her, we're not going to overlook the fact that this island is easily accessible by boat. Including by your boat. I heard that you and Jeanette didn't have a great relationship either."

Lyle's face reddened but he didn't shout. "I didn't have to be close to my sister to want justice done for my family." He thrust his jaw toward Nick and growled, "And you need to stop wasting your time poking around in my business."

Though Lyle wasn't shouting anymore, there must have been something Bear didn't appreciate in the man's surly voice. The little dog raced toward the burly fisherman, barking furiously.

"Control your mutt," Lyle demanded as he pulled back his leg, aiming his foot threateningly at Bear.

Nick grabbed the man and hauled him toward the door at the same time that Reese charged around the counter, putting himself between Lyle and Bear.

"We'll finish this outside," Nick said as he dragged the man out into the cold.

From the open doorway, Lyle pointed toward Bear and aimed his words at Kaylee. "You'd better keep that mutt away from me if you want it to stay healthy."

"That's it," Nick said. "We're going to the sheriff's station." The door swung closed and anything else Nick might have said was lost.

Kaylee walked around the counter and scooped up Bear, watching Nick hustle the man away through the window. "That's one seriously angry man," she said.

"Yeah," Reese agreed. "I hope Nick plans to measure his shoes."

With a shudder, Kaylee realized Reese thought Lyle might have been the person who'd been lurking outside of her cottage. That was a disquieting notion. Clearly sensing her worry, Bear licked her chin. For once, though, it didn't do much to make Kaylee feel better.

11

Reese watched Kaylee closely, concern clear in his blue eyes.

"I'm fine," she told him.

He studied her face a moment more, then appeared to accept what she said. "If you're okay with being here alone, I have a few shops along the street that I've got to check on. Every time I go in one, someone seems to have a problem with the plumbing or the electric or the heat."

"Then you'd best be on your way." She flapped a hand at him. "Thank you for the coffee."

"My pleasure." He grinned at her then, his eyes twinkling in a way that quickened Kaylee's pulse a bit. She was glad he couldn't see how much he affected her. *He'd think I was silly.*

She began fussing with some papers on the counter. "I'll see you later."

"Sure." His tone sounded puzzled, but Kaylee didn't look up again, and he left.

Kaylee released a pent-up breath. "I'm going to have to get a grip, Bear. I'm starting to act like some damsel in distress who swoons when a handsome man gives her a little attention."

Bear tilted his head and peered up at her curiously.

"Okay, fine, one specific handsome man."

Bear yipped in apparent agreement and Kaylee chuckled. *Having actual conversations with my dog and blushing every time Reese talks to me . . . I might need a little more sleep. I seem to be loopy today.* She finally decided that the stress of Lyle's animosity probably contributed to her nerves as well.

The door opened again, making Kaylee jump. She had a split

second of worry that Lyle was back, but a young couple came through the door, walking perfectly in step as they leaned into one another.

Kaylee beamed at them in relief. "Can I help you?"

"We're mostly browsing," the young woman said, "though I might find something pretty I can't do without." She gazed into the man's eyes.

"Of course," he said. "Anything you want."

Kaylee watched the couple weave through the shop displays, smiling at each other and speaking in low murmurs, and she felt her own mood lighten. *I guess I needed to be reminded of all the people enjoying life.*

Bear had stayed by Kaylee's side when the couple first came in, which she knew was because he'd sensed her disquiet, but after Kaylee began to relax, Bear trotted over to the young people as they stood near a display cooler.

"Oh, how sweet!" the woman cooed. "What a cutie." She shifted her gaze to Kaylee. "Can I pet him?"

Kaylee grinned. "He'd be disappointed if you didn't."

The customer bent and scratched Bear's ears. "I love the bow tie. He's adorable."

"Thank you. His name is Bear. He's my guard dog."

The couple laughed and gave Bear a few extra pats. Then the young woman picked a simple arrangement of pink tulips and carried it to the counter. "These ought to help me remember spring will be here—eventually."

"They're very cheery," Kaylee agreed.

The young woman passed her gaze across the sales floor, then frowned slightly. "I asked in a different shop about handmade soap and they said you had some, but I don't see it."

"I'm afraid I sold out of my stock earlier," Kaylee said. "Try asking at Between the Lines, the bookstore right there." She pointed out the window toward DeeDee's shop. "The owner actually makes the soap I carry here. She might have some in the back. She doesn't normally sell it from the store, but if she has any, I expect she'd sell it to you."

"Oh, I hope so. Thank you." The young woman paid for her flowers and the couple left, still arm in arm.

"We'll walk over and talk to DeeDee too," Kaylee said to Bear as he listened intently. "But I have to make a quick call first." Bear must have detected the stalling tone in her voice because he gave a disappointed sigh and collapsed on the bed behind the counter.

Kaylee picked up a list of flowers to preorder for a huge spring wedding. Some of the more exotic flowers had to be shipped in from overseas, so if she didn't make the order now, she couldn't be sure of delivery when she needed them. She dialed the wholesaler and placed the order.

"Anything else?" the operator asked.

Kaylee wondered whether she should get any of the flowers she commonly carried in the shop. Her supply was pretty good and she didn't want to misjudge these slow days and end up with a lot of flowers that died in the coolers. "No, I don't think so." She sighed. "This is the hardest time of year to anticipate accurate sales figures."

"For us too. I think we're all eager to see the end of winter and the start of spring."

Kaylee agreed, though she normally didn't mind winter on the island. As with many of Orcas Island's year-round inhabitants, she enjoyed the slower lifestyle. It gave them time to breathe and to notice the beautiful moments interspersed with the gray. But Jeanette's unsolved death was an extra cloud hanging over Turtle Cove, making the island's isolation in winter seem more menacing than peaceful.

As Kaylee ended the call, she felt antsy. "I think it's time for that walk, Bear." Bear leaped to his feet so quickly he practically seemed to levitate. Kaylee snapped on his leash and hung a sign on the door that said she would return within the hour. "Let's go talk to a lady about some soap."

The little dog yipped and danced as Kaylee opened the door, and they stepped out into the stiff February chill. The cold didn't seem to faze Bear at all, and he trotted along with his head high. Kaylee wished she could chase off the dark malaise she felt hanging over her as easily.

They'd covered about half the distance to the bookstore when the sky opened and a wave of drenching rain poured down, immediately soaking Kaylee to the skin despite her winter coat. She picked up her pace, though the downpour made it hard to see. Thankfully, she knew the way to Between the Lines with her eyes closed, which they nearly were.

She and Bear rushed through the door of the bookstore and Kaylee was delighted to see DeeDee Wilcox waiting for them with two large towels.

"I saw you coming." DeeDee handed Kaylee one towel and then crouched to dry Bear with the other one. "Would you like some hot chocolate? I'm afraid it's only the instant kind, not the fancy stuff Jess makes, but I've already got a pot of water on."

"That sounds fantastic." Kaylee slipped out of her jacket and hung it on the coat-tree. "I think I'm frozen clean through." She began toweling her dripping hair as she followed DeeDee to the counter. "But I can't imagine a better refuge in a storm than a bookstore."

"I hope everyone agrees with you," DeeDee said. "We could use the sales."

Soon Kaylee was perched on a stool behind the counter with another towel draped around her shoulders, a cup of hot chocolate in her hands, and Bear resting at her feet. He at least was completely dry. "How is it that you have so many towels here?"

"The girls," DeeDee said. "I've learned to be prepared for any catastrophe." DeeDee's two school-age daughters, Zoe and Polly, were a lively pair, and they kept their parents on their toes.

DeeDee sat on another stool, not far from Kaylee. "You came to check on that book you ordered, right? I'm so sorry to make you walk in the rain for nothing, but it hasn't come in yet."

"No problem," Kaylee said. "I'm eager to read it, but it's not pressing."

DeeDee raised her eyebrows. "I hope not. As I remember, it was a book on plant-based poisons. You're not planning to get into a side business, are you?"

Kaylee laughed. "Hardly, though I think learning more about the possible effects of plant-based toxins would be helpful in the work I do sometimes for the sheriff's department. That book contains all the most recent research on the subject. However, I mostly came over today because Bear needed a walk and I wanted to order more soap. I sold out this morning."

"That's amazing," DeeDee said. "You must have had a real run of customers."

"Not so much. I sold them all to a pair of ladies who wanted them for the senior center in Eastsound."

"Oh, that's kind of them." DeeDee shifted a little on her stool. "I only have a few bars here, but I made a new batch recently so I'll bring you some tomorrow. I did sell a bar a little bit ago to the sweetest couple who came in and asked for one specifically. They said the nice lady at the flower shop sent them. I wondered if you had run out."

"I hope they didn't get too drenched in this rain."

"If they did, I'm not sure they'd mind. They seemed to be completely caught up in one another. It made me remember my early days with Andy. We were so young."

"You're not exactly elderly now," Kaylee said with a laugh.

"True, and Andy can still surprise me with romantic evenings, but we've got two kids. It's hard to find time for romance when you're rushing to make it to dance class or softball practice."

Kaylee thought wistfully that she wouldn't mind any kind of romance before she sternly told herself not to be silly. She wasn't exactly lonely. She had dear friends in Turtle Cove, and she had Bear. And she loved her work. But still, sometimes she longed to go walking hand in hand on the beach or kiss someone under the stars. For some reason, her imagination planted Reese in that spot and Kaylee jumped in surprise, her cheeks flaming.

"Something wrong?" DeeDee asked.

Kaylee shook her head. "I didn't get enough sleep last night. It's made me edgy and weird all day."

"I have those nights sometimes. What kept you up? Was it the whole murder thing?"

"Murder?" Kaylee gawked at her in surprise. "Surely you're not jumping the gun too. It's just as likely that Jeanette's death was an accident as murder."

"Which means it's a mystery." DeeDee laughed. "And if we have a mystery in Turtle Cove, who else would be in the middle of it?"

"Roz Corzo, in this case." Kaylee sipped her cocoa, then relented. "As it turns out, I have been involved a little, but only because the sheriff's department needed some plant evidence analyzed. And also, Roz thinks I can clear her name and find out what really happened to Jeanette."

"You've done it before."

"Maybe, but Roz called me nosy, which I am not."

"How dare she?" DeeDee's smirk indicated that she was being facetious.

Kaylee made a face at her friend's teasing, then asked, "What have you heard about the whole thing?"

"That Roz and this woman were having a drunken party on Roz's boat in the middle of the storm. Roz passed out and the woman fell overboard. And the police are involved because Roz was criminally negligent in taking a boat out in that weather." DeeDee's tone indicated that she didn't entirely believe the rumors.

Kaylee shook her head. "Roz and Jeanette weren't drinking alcohol. Roz passed out because of some tea that had been heavily doctored with valerian root."

"Valerian?" DeeDee echoed. "I'm not familiar with that."

"It's commonly used as a natural sedative. All parts of it can promote sleep, but the root especially. Apparently Jeanette was very into herbalism, and there's evidence that she was drying it in her room at the Northern Lights Inn."

"Weird."

"And confusing." Kaylee explained about Smith Hooper, as well as the dead woman's ex-husband and brother. "It's a complete muddle. And on top of everything, a coworker of Jeanette's came over at her invitation, and now she wants to play Nancy Drew with me."

"I can't blame anyone for that. If I didn't have a husband and kids, I'd be asking to play Nancy Drew with you too." Then DeeDee's expression became serious. "I am worried about the brother though, especially if he's aiming some of that anger at you or Bear. He sounds dangerous."

"I fear he might be," Kaylee said. "But his anger at Bear was probably fleeting. I expect he's forgotten all about it by now." At least she hoped he had. "Still, it seems like he wouldn't draw so much attention to himself if he were the killer. That's not smart."

DeeDee snorted and gestured at the rows of bookracks in the shop. "We are surrounded by true-crime books that generally make it clear that most criminals aren't particularly smart."

The door to the bookshop opened and another sodden refugee

from the storm came in, his boots squishing as he walked.

"Hello, Reese." DeeDee hopped up. "Let me get you a towel."

"Thanks," he said. "I don't think I knew it was supposed to rain today, and I left my umbrella in the truck."

DeeDee handed him a towel. "It's winter in Washington. It's supposed to rain every day."

Reese spotted Kaylee as he began toweling his hair. "I see you got caught in the rain too, so I'm not alone in misjudging."

"Definitely not," Kaylee said. "Bear and I started across the street with no rain and then the sky tried to drown us."

"Glad you made it here alive," he said with a grin, then turned to DeeDee. "You wanted me to check on the electrical panel, right?"

DeeDee nodded. "The lights keep flickering in the storeroom. I've changed the bulbs, so that's not it. I thought maybe the panel could be the issue."

"I'll check everything," Reese said as the front door opened again.

When DeeDee went to greet the soggy new arrival with yet another towel, Reese raised an eyebrow at Kaylee. "How many towels does that woman keep in her shop?"

"Enough, I hope," Kaylee said. "I wish I hadn't used so much of her stash."

"Maybe the rain will stop soon." Reese glanced toward the window with a frown. "When it downpours like this, it rarely lasts long." He folded the towel he'd used. "I wish it hadn't rained."

"Why?"

"When I talked to Nick, he hadn't yet compared Lyle's shoes to the prints outside your house." He scowled at the window again. "But now the rain will ruin any chance of identifying them, unless Nick somehow got to your place ahead of the rain."

"I doubt it matters. Lyle had no reason to hang out at my cottage. He hasn't shown any sign of thinking *I* killed his sister.

I'm telling you, Reese, it was almost certainly one of my neighbors taking a walk." Kaylee wished desperately that she felt as sure as she was trying to sound.

"Either way, I thought I might come home with you this evening and check out the property before you go in the house. It doesn't hurt to be careful."

"Don't worry about it. I'm fine. If Bear acts the least bit twitchy, I'll call Nick. I promise."

Reese didn't seem happy, but he didn't press her. "I suppose I should go work on DeeDee's lights and then finish the rest of the small jobs along the street." He brightened and his expression grew mischievous. "Say, here's something you might find interesting: I have to go over to the wharf after that. I have a little job to do on a boat there."

Kaylee eyed him suspiciously. "Any boat I might be familiar with?"

"Could be," he said. "Pop Ronson is having trouble with a pump, and I promised to come fix it. You want to come along? I can always use an assistant to hand me tools. It makes me appear more successful."

Kaylee responded to his teasing smile with one of her own. *Would I care to come along for the perfect opportunity to pump Pop Ronson for more information about Jeanette's death?* She told herself that spending more time with Reese had nothing to do with it. "Count me in."

12

The pounding rain soon tapered off to a drizzle, and Kaylee knew she should return to the shop. She was folding damp towels when DeeDee joined her at the counter after helping a few customers.

"Are you heading out?" DeeDee asked.

"I don't want to miss any of my own customers," Kaylee said. "And I think we can get back without drowning now." She bit her lip, considering, then plunged ahead. "I hate to ask another favor right after you saved us from the monsoon, but do you think I could bring Bear over this afternoon for a little while? Reese asked me to go with him on a job."

DeeDee raised both eyebrows high. "He did?" She grinned, and Kaylee felt a blush creeping over her face again. "You could be helping him in the storeroom right now. Why wait?"

"His job this afternoon is related to the investigation into Jeanette's death," Kaylee whispered.

"The investigation you're barely involved in?" DeeDee's grin widened as Kaylee felt more heat creeping up her face. "You are too fun to tease. It's fine for Bear to stay for a while. The girls are coming to the shop after school. They'll be thrilled to find him here."

"And he'll love seeing them." Through the window, Kaylee saw the rain had either stopped or nearly so. "We'd better make a break for it. Who knows if it'll start pouring again?"

DeeDee gathered up the damp towels. "I'll see you later. And I'll check on that book order. It should have been here by now."

"No hurry," Kaylee said as she scooped up Bear and walked

around the counter. "I'm more in need of the soap."

"Oh, thanks for reminding me. I'll give you the bars I have to tide you over until I can get you more tomorrow. Hang on a minute." DeeDee carried the towels to the back, then returned quickly with the soap in a small paper sack.

"Thanks a bunch," Kaylee said, accepting the bag and heading for the door with Bear in tow. "See you in a bit. And hopefully less soggy next time."

Kaylee had only one customer between the time she reached her shop and when Reese showed up well past noon. On top of that, the visitor didn't buy anything—he merely stood at the counter and complained about the weather. Kaylee could sympathize, but weather wasn't exactly something the shopkeepers of Turtle Cove could fix.

By the time Reese came in on the next wave of rain, Kaylee was sweeping again. Reese saw the broom in her hands and gazed down at his boots. "Sorry, I'm making a mess."

"That's okay. This was boredom sweeping. I think we've reached the part of winter where I'm not appreciating the slower pace so much."

Reese laughed. "You and every shopkeeper I've seen today." He gestured toward the empty sales floor. "Think you can sneak away?"

"I can, but I thought maybe we could eat first. Have you had lunch? I could make sandwiches and heat up some soup."

"That would be great," he said. "I was thinking that I'd enjoy something hot other than coffee. If I have much more caffeine, I'm going to vibrate into pieces."

Kaylee led Reese to the kitchen area of the shop to eat, and Bear trotted along behind them, happy to be following two of his favorite people to one of his favorite rooms.

"If you'll point me in the right direction, I can heat up the soup while you start the sandwiches," Reese offered.

Kaylee opened a cupboard and handed him a can of clam chowder. "It seems like a chowder day to me."

"Me too."

After giving Reese a pot for the soup, she began collecting deli meat and cheese from the refrigerator. "Did you find the problem at the bookstore?"

"Loose wiring," he answered as he cranked the can opener. "Good thing she called me. Loose wiring is one of the major causes of house fires."

Kaylee grimaced. "Great, now I'll be paranoid every time one of my lights flickers."

He glanced up sharply. "Does that happen often? I've checked the wiring out at the cottage a number of times."

Kaylee held up her hand. "I was kidding. Really, the only time the lights flicker is during storms."

"Never kid about wiring around a handyman."

"Yes sir." Kaylee began slathering slices of thick brown bread with spicy mustard. "I appreciate you letting me come along to Pop Ronson's. Even if I don't learn anything about Jeanette, it'll be good to get out of the shop. I love The Flower Patch, but it's been a little depressing with no foot traffic."

"Spring is coming." He stirred the soup. "Have you thought of where you're going to put Mom's bulbs?"

Kaylee began piling meat on the sandwiches. "Honestly, I haven't given it a thought. I've done some sketches of changes I might make to the flower beds around the cottage, but nothing set in stone."

"Seems to me you gardeners are always tinkering," he said. "My mom is the same way." He tapped the spoon on the side of the steaming pot. "I think this is ready."

"Perfect timing." Kaylee put the sandwiches on plates. "These are done too." As she was putting away the deli meat, she *accidentally* dropped a slice of roast beef on the floor and Bear pounced on it with gusto.

Reese laughed. "I thought you were the one who always says Bear gets too many treats."

"I do," Kaylee admitted. "But he loves roast beef. I try not to eat it unless I share a teeny bit. But he has no idea I dropped it on purpose. I can't have him thinking I've gone soft on his treat rations." The roast beef gone, Bear sat up in his most winsome pose, but she shook a finger at him. "You've had enough."

Kaylee and Reese settled at the small kitchen table and ate in companionable silence. Kaylee appreciated that they could be quiet together without it becoming awkward, and it gave her a chance to steal a few glances his way. She enjoyed the way his broad shoulders filled out the soft flannel shirt he wore. They were only friends, but that didn't mean she couldn't appreciate what a handsome guy he was. And kind and loyal. With a silent inner sigh, Kaylee wondered how it would be if they were more than friends.

Realizing that she was daydreaming, Kaylee sat up straight, shaking off such silly thoughts.

"Is something wrong?" Reese asked.

"No, nothing." *Don't blush. Don't blush. Don't blush.* "Do you think I used too much mustard?"

"Tastes perfect to me."

"Good." Kaylee glanced at the untouched half sandwich on her plate and realized she'd overestimated her hunger after all. *I'll wrap up the other half for later.* She glanced over at Reese's empty plate. "Ready to go?"

After dropping Bear off at Between the Lines, Kaylee hopped into Reese's truck and they drove the couple minutes to the ferry parking lot. Kaylee was happy to see the rain had stopped, though the heavy clouds above them suggested it could restart at any time.

Reese handed Kaylee a tool belt. "This should help you appear official."

"Sure, that ought to fool him." Kaylee wrapped the belt around her waist, but there weren't enough holes in the leather to strap it particularly tight, so the belt hung low on her hips.

Reese hefted the heavy toolbox and headed for the dock with Kaylee following behind, hitching up the tool belt every few yards. *How do people wear these things?* It was much more cumbersome than the apron she carried her gardening supplies in when she was working in the yard.

When they reached Pop Ronson's boat, Reese bellowed, "Ahoy!"

Pop glared down at them, his expression suspicious. He pointed at Kaylee. "What's she doing here?"

"She's my assistant," Reese said. Then he winked at Pop. "She'll brighten up your boat a bit."

The older man harrumphed, but he didn't argue. "As long as you fix the pump, I don't care if you bring along the whole town."

Kaylee followed Reese aboard, and she swiftly saw the full power of Reese Holt's charm as he laid it on the gruff boat captain. He soon had Pop chuckling over a joke about barnacles, and then he turned to Kaylee. "Can you stay up here? I don't think there will be room for you in the hold. It gets tight down there."

"Whatever you think," Kaylee said. She smiled brightly at Pop, and to her surprise, he smiled back—not a big grin or anything, but an improvement on the suspicious scowl he'd been giving her.

When Reese squeezed down into the works of the boat, Kaylee scanned the cabin. "This is nice."

"Isn't it?" Pop frowned at the cabin as if it were failing him somehow. "I don't understand why I don't get more business."

"Hard time of year," Kaylee answered, hitching the tool belt up again.

Pop chuckled. "You ought to take that thing off, missy. Pretty soon it's going to fall on the floor."

Kaylee doubted that, but she wasn't going to argue. "I think you're right." She started to unstrap it. "If I had one more hole in the belt it would be better."

Pop held out his hand. "I could do that for you. I've got an awl around here somewhere."

Kaylee wasn't sure how Reese would feel about him damaging the tool belt, but she hated to risk spoiling the older man's softening mood. "That's kind of you."

Pop's cheeks reddened slightly as he accepted the belt. "Nothing to it." He began rummaging in drawers built into the cabin wall.

Kaylee figured now was as good a time as any to broach the sensitive topic she'd come to investigate. "The last time we talked, you said something that made me wonder."

Pop made a noncommittal grunt, his attention on a drawer full of odds and ends, most of which Kaylee couldn't identify.

"How did you know Roz and Jeanette had been drinking tea? Everyone else seemed to think they were drinking alcohol."

Another grunt, then Pop frowned at her and slammed the drawer. He plopped down on one of the benches in the cabin with an awl in his hand. "Roz doesn't drink. Besides, I heard those two talking."

"Out in the sound?"

"Don't be dim," he growled as he worked the tool into the leather belt. "When they were still on land. They had to pass my boat to get to Roz's. Corzo was complaining about the cold, and I heard Jeanette saying she had some new herbal tea they could drink to warm up."

What Pop was saying sounded completely reasonable, but Kaylee got the distinct impression that it wasn't strictly true.

He hopped up suddenly and thrust the belt toward her. "That should do you. I have to go talk to the harbormaster about something. You tell Reese to leave an invoice for the work."

"Of course, and thank you for fixing the belt," Kaylee said, wondering at Pop's sudden hurry to get away from her. What exactly in their conversation had triggered the reaction?

Kaylee stood near the rail to watch the older man scurry away, his heavy boots thudding down the dock. When he was out of sight, she pivoted to view the cabin. *He* did *leave me here. How could I not poke around a little?*

She'd seen the contents of most of the drawers when Pop was rooting for the awl, so she didn't bother with them. Instead, she sat down on a bench next to a small, fold-down desk. The desktop was a haphazard mess of papers. Kaylee leaned close to see if she could make anything of the paperwork without actually disturbing anything. It all seemed to be the normal sort of things—mostly bills along with some personal letters.

She scooted even closer to the desk, but bumped the edge, jostling the fold-down surface and sending half of the papers fluttering down to the floor.

"Oh dear." There was no way Pop wouldn't notice that she'd messed with his things now.

As she cleaned up the mess, she spotted a thick business envelope. *In for a penny, in for a pound.* She picked it up and peered inside. The envelope was full of money, a lot of it.

Kaylee piled the rest of the papers on the desk before counting the money in the envelope: $5,000 in hundred-dollar bills. *Why does Pop have an envelope full of so much cash?* She supposed it could be a payment for a recent trip out. She had no idea how much it might cost to rent a big boat like Pop's, but it seemed odd that someone would pay for it in cash.

Kaylee took a photo of the packed envelope with her phone, then replaced the envelope on the desk. She walked to the hatch leading to the hold. "Reese!"

His face popped up below her, a streak of grease across his nose that she found endearing somehow. "Everything okay?"

"Pop left. He said to leave an invoice when you're done," she said. "And I'm going to see if Roz is on her boat. I have some questions for her."

"Sounds good," Reese said. "If you're not back when I'm done, I'll come find you."

Kaylee was glad to find Roz on her boat, though Roz was less thrilled to see Kaylee.

"I thought you'd have figured out Jeanette's murder by now," the boat captain grumbled. "I expect to be carted off in cuffs any minute. It's making it hard to work."

"I don't think the sheriff's department works that way," Kaylee said. "They don't arrest a lot of innocent people."

With a grunt, Roz folded her arms over her chest. "You wanted something?"

"As a boat captain, would you ever have $5,000 in cash on your boat?" Kaylee asked. "Is that a reasonable sum to get from a client?"

Roz pulled on her lower lip as she thought about the question. "That would be a lot. I suppose I might get that much if I were taking a retainer for a full season of regular fishing trips, especially if they were group trips. But I don't get cash. People don't want to deal in cash as there's not enough paper trail if they don't like my services."

"I found an envelope with exactly that much in hundred-dollar bills on Pop Ronson's desk," Kaylee said.

Roz dropped her arms and stood straighter. "That doesn't make sense. Pop hasn't been busy enough to take in that kind of money. No one has. Nobody's interested in boating this time of year, so we plan ahead for the lack of income."

"So could that be the money he stockpiled for this lean time?" Kaylee asked.

"Why? We all have bank accounts. We pay bills out of the accounts the same as everyone else." Then she shoved her hands into the pockets of her worn jeans. "Unless Pop needs money for something and doesn't want anyone to find out."

"I wondered about that." Kaylee's gaze swept Roz's cabin. It was neater than Pop's, but not particularly larger or fancier. "Pop complains about how you always get more clients than he does. Why do you think that is?"

"Ask me a tough question." Roz snorted. "I keep my boat clean. Pop's tub smells of dead fish all the time. On hot days, it can be positively repulsive to be moored next to it."

Kaylee hadn't noticed much of a smell, but maybe the odor was less noticeable in the frigid weather. She did agree, however, that Pop's boat was messy compared to Roz's. "Thanks for the information," she said finally. "I ought to get back to join Reese."

Roz folded her arms again. "I hope you're working on more than your love life."

"You're such a grouch," Kaylee snapped. "If you weren't, people would actually want to help you." Immediately she regretted it. Why had she said that?

To her surprise, Roz laughed uproariously. "Good for you, Kaylee. I earned that." Her face softened. "I'm scared, that's all. Tell Reese I said hi."

"Hopefully soon you won't have anything to be afraid of," Kaylee said, then headed to Pop's boat with questions about the money still swirling in her mind. Was Pop involved in something illegal? Something someone would pay a lot for in cash? And if so, had Jeanette figured it out?

As she climbed aboard Pop's fishing boat, the older man burst out of the cabin. "What were you doing poking around in my stuff? Don't think I didn't notice!"

"I apologize, I accidentally knocked your papers on the floor," Kaylee said. "Space is cramped in there. I did, however, wonder about the envelope full of hundred-dollar bills when I picked it up. If you haven't had much business, how did you come by all that money?"

"I don't have to tell you anything!" the older man bellowed.

The sound must have carried down to Reese, because the next thing Kaylee knew, he was stepping between her and Pop. "You don't need to shout."

"She was poking in my private things," Pop said. "Then she had the nerve to interrogate me about it. She's got no right to my business."

"You're right," Kaylee said calmly, though she was grateful for Reese providing a buffer between her and the angry man. "It's your business. But it's something I have to tell the sheriff's department. It's a little suspicious that a woman died mysteriously on a boat that normally moors right next to yours, and you just happen to have an envelope packed full of hundred-dollar bills. The sheriff is going to want to hear about it."

"You don't understand." All the anger seemed to drain out of Pop, leaving him slumped and miserable. "I never killed anyone. It's true that I got that money from Jeanette, but I never hurt her. She *gave* it to me. And she promised me a lot more, so I would have been crazy to hurt her."

"Why would she give you an envelope full of cash?" Kaylee asked.

He raised his head, his face drawn. "Because she was planning her death."

13

"You're saying Jeanette Colson's death was suicide?" Kaylee asked, surprise making her voice louder than she intended.

Pop shushed her. "I don't know what it was." His eyes darted toward Roz's boat nervously. "Can we get off the deck to talk about this? I'd rather not have my business shouted to the world."

"It's not your business we're interested in," Reese said. "And I'm not sure we're the ones you should be telling it to." He shot a glance at Kaylee. "We should probably call the sheriff's department."

Pop waved that off. "No, no. Let's not get hasty. I don't mind telling the two of you, but I'm not sure we ought to get the sheriff's department involved."

"Why not?" Reese asked. "Have you done something wrong?"

"Wrong? No, I don't think so." Pop shifted restlessly, his gaze again darting toward Roz's boat. "Illegal? Maybe."

Kaylee rested her hand on Reese's arm. "We should go to the cabin and hear what Pop has to say. Then we can decide whether to get Nick involved."

Reese clearly wasn't completely comfortable with that idea but he finally nodded.

Once in the cabin, Pop reached into a mini refrigerator and pulled out a bottle of water with shaking hands. He sank onto one of the benches and drank the water in gulps. Kaylee and Reese sat on the bench across from him and waited.

Finally, Pop hunched over with the empty bottle clenched between both hands, staring down at it as he spoke. "Jeanette Colson told me that she planned to fake her own death. She said things were getting too complicated in her life, so she wanted to start a new one. She had the whole plan in place, and she needed someone to give her a ride from Roz's boat out on the sound back to the docks."

"And she gave you an envelope stuffed with money in exchange," Kaylee said.

Pop's head bobbed. "She gave me the money Thursday and told me there would be another envelope when I brought her here on Friday night."

"How would you be able to find Roz's boat?" Reese asked. "Even if they didn't go out far, it could take a while to find them."

"She called after Roz passed out and gave me the GPS coordinates. I headed out there straight away, but she never came out on deck. I yelled for her and waited a solid half hour, but she never showed. The wind was picking up and I wasn't comfortable with my boat being so close to Roz's tub in that kind of chop, so I left. I figured half the fee was better than nothing, and I sure as heck wasn't going to give anything back because she got cold feet."

"Did you try calling her phone?" Kaylee asked.

"It went to voice mail."

"Why didn't you tell all this to the police when the woman went missing?" Reese asked.

"I don't want to be involved," Pop said. "I don't think what I did was illegal, but I'm not sure, and I thought it was better to keep my mouth shut." He glared at Reese and Kaylee. "And you two should too."

"That's not going to happen." Reese pulled out his phone. "You're going to tell Deputy Durham exactly what you told us, or we're going to tell him for you. And I promise the sheriff's department will be easier on you if it comes from you directly."

Pop narrowed his eyes. "Not much of a choice."

"Yeah," Reese said. "That's life sometimes."

As Reese made the call, Kaylee leaned forward. "Why would Jeanette want to fake her death? Did she indicate what was complicating her life?"

Pop shook his head. "I didn't ask for details. The money was good, and I didn't mind seeing Roz's face when she found out her *friend* wasn't a friend at all."

Kaylee flinched at the venom in the man's tone, but she didn't ask any more questions. She doubted Pop Ronson had any more answers. Still, why would Jeanette want to run away from her life? Could she have been afraid of something? So afraid that she'd be willing to pay thousands of dollars to escape? "And where did Jeanette get all that money?"

Kaylee didn't realize she'd spoken the last question aloud until Reese answered. "Savings, maybe."

Kaylee supposed that was possible, depending on Jeanette's job and what it might pay. At least she knew someone she could ask, which she'd do after Nick came to take over with Pop.

When the deputy arrived a few minutes later, Kaylee and Reese met him on deck and filled him in.

"Thanks," Nick said when they had finished. "I need to speak to Pop alone. I may have some follow-up questions for you later."

"Should we stay here?" Reese asked.

Nick shook his head. "I know where to find you."

Kaylee was grateful for her coat as she returned to the parking lot with Reese, although the rain seemed done for the day, and she thought the temperature might even have risen a bit.

"What did you think of Pop's story?" she asked as they walked.

"I believe him," Reese said. "Pop is the sort of guy who would take money for something like that without asking too many questions."

"What if he did pick Jeanette up, and she didn't have the

second payment to give him?" Kaylee asked. "Is he the kind of guy who might throw her overboard?"

"Not intentionally," Reese said. "Pop is an opportunist, but I can't see him as a killer."

"Maybe it was an accident," Kaylee said. "The water was rough. A transfer like that would be difficult. If he was involved in Jeanette's death, he'd probably be scared enough to lie about it."

"That isn't impossible, but I'm still not convinced. He's not exactly warm and fuzzy, but I can't believe he'd be so heartless as to leave the family wondering if Jeanette was murdered."

"None of the people connected to this case seem heartless. That's the problem," Kaylee said. "I can't see any of the people in Jeanette's life as killers." *With the possible exception of her brother. That man is dangerously full of rage.*

Kaylee realized Reese was staring at her quizzically. "What?" she asked.

"I was wondering what you're thinking," he said. "You seem worried."

"It's Lyle Colson. I could see him as capable of murder. Plus he owns a boat. What if Jeanette called him as a backup? Or what if he'd simply been following Roz's boat and took advantage of Jeanette's plan to kill her himself?"

"I think Nick needs to find out what Lyle was doing while someone was tromping around your cottage."

Kaylee groaned. "Let's not get back to that. I'm sure that wasn't Lyle. He had no reason to hang out at my cottage. If he was going to watch someone, I'd expect it would have been Roz." Then she gave Reese's shoulder a playful swat. "And thanks, by the way. I'd forgotten all about that until you reminded me. I can't wait to go home in the dark again."

"Sorry about that," Reese said, though he didn't sound particularly contrite. "I'd feel a lot better if you'd let me follow you home and check out the cottage and grounds before you turn in for the night."

Kaylee almost refused again, but she knew she'd feel better too if Reese checked. She wanted to be independent, but that didn't mean she needed to be stupid. "Thank you," she said finally. "I'd appreciate it. I'll even fix you some dinner."

His face brightened at that. "Two meals with Kaylee Bleu in one day? Now things are truly looking up."

She laughed. "Because that sandwich and canned soup we had for lunch was gourmet cooking at its finest."

"Clearly you don't know what I usually eat," he said.

They reached his truck, and he lowered the tailgate and put his toolbox into the bed. "Let me give you a lift to the bookstore to collect Bear. Are you going home straight after?"

"I should go to the shop for about an hour," she said. "Tomorrow is Friday, and it's a busy day for pickup orders so I've got to put together a couple of arrangements. Does that work for you?"

"That's perfect," he said. "I got a text while we were on Pop's boat. Art Attack has a dripping faucet and if I can fix it before we leave, I should be done with all the shops. Then tomorrow I can work on furnaces in some of the houses outside of town. Honestly, I think people broke things simply because I left the island for a few days."

"You're certainly in high demand," Kaylee teased.

A few minutes later, Reese dropped Kaylee off in front of Between the Lines with a promise to pick her up at The Flower Patch an hour later. She entered the bookshop and was greeted by an enthusiastic Bear, who now sported a jaunty hat to go with his bow tie. Kaylee suspected that was Polly's handiwork.

Sure enough, Polly came running out right behind him. "Don't you think he's handsome in that hat?"

"He certainly is," Kaylee agreed. "But I'm going to have to take him so we can finish up at The Flower Patch and go home." She saw DeeDee coming out of a row of bookshelves and waved at her. "Thanks for watching Bear."

"Anytime," DeeDee said. "Bear is the best entertainment in the world for Polly. And Zoe would have loved playing with him as well if she hadn't had a yearbook staff meeting after school."

"Can Bear come over tomorrow?" Polly asked.

Kaylee gave the little girl a hug. "Probably not. Bear has to help me at my shop."

Polly pouted for an instant before her natural good humor washed the expression away. She dropped to her knees to take off Bear's hat. "You can wear it again the next time you visit," she promised him as she kissed the top of his head. Then she looked up at Kaylee in alarm. "I promised Bear a biscuit for playing the little kid in my game. I forgot to give him one. Can I do that?"

Though Bear certainly didn't need more treats, Kaylee knew it was good that Polly wanted to follow through on her promises. "Sure, I'll wait."

Polly popped up to stand. "Great. Come on, Bear."

While Polly and Bear ran to the storeroom for a treat, DeeDee poked Kaylee gently. "So, are you going to tell me how the afternoon went?"

DeeDee's eyes sparkled with mischief, and Kaylee suspected she was asking about Kaylee's time with Reese. Instead, Kaylee quickly filled her in on what she'd learned about Pop Ronson and Jeanette.

DeeDee's eyes got wider and wider as Kaylee told her about the envelope of cash and about Jeanette's plan. "You don't think he killed her, do you?" she whispered. "He's been in a few times. He's a little grumpy, but he doesn't seem like a murderer."

"I don't believe he is," Kaylee said. She stopped talking

when Polly and Bear returned from the storeroom. "Okay, Bear. Time to head out."

DeeDee jumped and held up a hand. "Wait, I forgot. Andy ran by the house and got some soap for you. He dropped it off earlier. Hold on."

"That was nice of him." Kaylee snapped on Bear's leash, then stood, her gaze idly moving to the front window where a man stared in. The bright lights of the shop deepened the late-afternoon darkness outside, and Kaylee couldn't make out who the man was. But when he saw her, he jumped back from the window and rushed away.

Kaylee was still frowning at the window when DeeDee brought the soap.

"What's the matter?" DeeDee asked.

"Nothing." Kaylee took the box of soap. "I'm creeping myself out. I'll see you later."

As Kaylee walked Bear to the shop, she pushed away thoughts of the unidentified trespasser and pointedly concentrated on Pop Ronson. Clearly she wasn't the only one having trouble seeing the grumpy old sea captain as a killer. Still, the weather had been rough that night, and Pop admitted to not being comfortable with how close together the boats were. What if he'd never had a chance to collect the second envelope of cash because Jeanette hadn't survived moving from one boat to the next? In that kind of weather, if she fell in the water, he might not have been able to find her.

Questions continued to spin in Kaylee's mind through her last hour at the shop. When Reese arrived, Kaylee was staring at three small arrangements, with no memory of having made them in her distraction. Reese followed Kaylee and Bear as they drove back to Wildflower Cottage, and she was surprised at how much better she felt knowing that he was going to be there when she got home.

"I can't get used to that, Bear," she said aloud in the car. "I'll become one of those frightened women who is constantly calling for help every time the wind whistles in the eaves. I won't do that."

Once home, Kaylee quickly thawed some homemade beef barley soup she'd frozen weeks earlier and popped a loaf of crusty bread in the oven to warm while the soup heated on the stove. "I hope you don't mind soup again," she said to Reese when he walked into the kitchen after checking all the window locks.

"This time of year, I could eat soup for every meal." He inhaled deeply near the stove. "And that smells amazing."

"It's one of Grandma's recipes," she said. "I loved her beef barley soup when I was a kid."

Reese peered around the kitchen. "Anything I can do to help?"

"I think the bread in the oven is probably warm enough. Could you slice it?"

They pointedly talked about things unrelated to murder or intruders as they ate dinner. Reese entertained Kaylee with stories of his talk for the club on the mainland. "I don't think half the audience knew a thing about boats," he said, chuckling. "I nearly lost it when one of the men asked if I could tell him where he could buy life jackets in a more appealing color than 'that ghastly orange.'" His imitation of the man's horrified tone made Kaylee giggle.

After helping wash the dishes, Reese took a walk around the property before meeting Kaylee on the front porch to give her the all clear.

"Everything is secure," he said. "I still think you need to be careful, especially after dark. Pay attention to Bear. If he's upset, promise you'll run in the *other* direction."

"I'll be careful," she promised, trying for a light teasing tone. "Now go on before you make me a nervous wreck."

"I don't want you to be scared," Reese said, his voice still solemn. "I want you to be safe."

"And I will be. I promise." She pushed Reese toward his truck.

He relented, letting her move him along. "I'll come by the shop tomorrow if I can. If not, I'll text."

"I'm fine, Reese," she insisted.

He stood at the door of his truck, studying her as if he thought he'd find something important in her face. Something about his expression brought heat to her cheeks. Finally Reese nodded and quietly bid her good night. She watched him drive away, her mind unsettled.

As she returned to the house with Bear by her side, she said, "No one is interested in hurting me. Right, Bear?"

Bear yipped in agreement, but Kaylee locked the door behind her without her usual sense of warmth and safety.

"I'm fine," she scolded herself. "Completely fine."

Now if only she could believe it.

14

Kaylee felt so tired Friday morning, she was surprised she didn't need to rest on her way from the car to the shop door.

Mary took one look at Kaylee when she entered and shoved a mug of coffee into her hands. "What happened?" she asked.

Kaylee took a long sip of the coffee, relishing the warmth of it after braving the cold morning. "I didn't sleep very well."

"Why?" Mary asked. "Surely you're not that worried about Roz."

"No, though that would make me sound like a better person than the truth." She took another sip and sighed. "Someone was in my yard the night before last. They don't seem to have come close to the house or anything, but they freaked Bear out. And both Nick and Reese made a big deal about it."

Mary raised her eyebrows. "Reese is back? Good. And I'm not surprised they made a big deal about this. You're out there alone."

"I'm not alone. I have Bear." Kaylee ignored Mary's laughter. "Plus, I'm hardly a helpless damsel in distress. All they did with their warnings and fretting was make me jumpy. Do you have any idea how many sounds an old house can make, especially on a windy night?"

"Yeah, that I can understand. But the guys meant well."

"Tell that to my sleep deprivation headache." Kaylee walked to a spot behind the counter and began tidying the display of soap.

"Hopefully the coffee will kick in soon," Mary said.

"I'll be fine." Then Kaylee glanced toward the front windows and groaned. "Or not."

Roz stormed through the door. "Pop Ronson killed Jeanette?"

Bear peeked around the counter at Roz, then ducked back

behind Kaylee's legs. Even her intrepid protector didn't want to deal with Roz.

"What are you talking about?" Kaylee asked, waving off Mary, who was beginning to puff up in indignation at Roz's rude entrance.

"You know exactly what I'm talking about, and you'd better fill me in," Roz ordered. "And don't play innocent with me. Why did Nick haul Pop away yesterday? And what was with all those questions you asked me? If you've found Jeanette's killer, you owe me answers."

"I don't think Pop killed anyone," Kaylee said calmly. "But he did have some information about her disappearance."

Roz narrowed her eyes. "What kind of information?"

"Pop says that Jeanette paid him thousands of dollars to come and pick her up from your boat and bring her to land. He knew she planned to drug you."

"Why?" Roz demanded.

"He said she wanted to disappear and start a new life. So she was faking her death."

"And leaving me behind to be named the killer?" The anger had faded from Roz's voice, leaving her sounding forlorn instead. "I thought she was my friend."

Kaylee had never seen Roz appear so human and vulnerable. She felt terrible for her, something she'd never thought possible.

Mary gently touched Roz's arm, her countenance completely changed. "Can I get you something, Roz? A glass of water or some coffee?"

Roz stared at her as if struggling to understand what Mary was offering. Then she nodded. "Coffee would be good. Black."

As Mary hurried away, Kaylee spoke gently. "Jeanette must have been fleeing from something pretty serious to do that. Do you have any idea what it might have been?"

Roz shook her head. Her eyes filled, and she rubbed them angrily with the edge of her gloved hands. "Maybe something to do with Bart. If he was counting on them getting back together and Jeanette changed her mind, she might have been scared."

"Would Jeanette have had reason to be afraid of Bart?" Kaylee asked.

"Not that I'm aware of. Although when they were together, Jeanette complained about Bart's jealousy. She said he could get crazy sometimes."

"Was he ever violent?" Kaylee asked.

"I never thought so, but Jeanette seemed honestly frightened a few times." Roz ran her hand though her gray curls. "Though now I have to wonder if anything she ever told me was true. Clearly our friendship wasn't real."

"But if she was being honest . . ."

"If he thought they were getting together and learned there was another guy, he wouldn't have reacted well."

"Was there another guy?"

Roz groaned and buried her face in her hands. "I couldn't tell you. It's like she wasn't even my friend."

Mary came back with coffee in a lidded foam cup. Kaylee felt a smile tug at the corner of her mouth. Mary was kind enough to share coffee, but not so kind that she wanted to encourage Roz to hang around.

Roz took the coffee without comment and stared at the cup. "Come to think of it, Jeanette was acting funny about work. Maybe she was involved with someone there? If Bart found out she was, that might have scared her."

"Acting funny?" Kaylee repeated. "Funny how?"

Roz shrugged. "Jeanette was a talker, but when it came to her job, she didn't seem to want to discuss it at all. She said it was dull, but fine. A way to pay the bills." Roz paused and took a sip. "Jeanette enjoyed talking about *everything*, so why would she clam up about her job?"

Kaylee thought Roz's theory might be a bit of a stretch, but she did have a possible source to ask about it. She didn't mention it to Roz, though, and merely consoled her until she finally left the shop, coffee still in hand. As soon as Roz was outside, Bear trotted out from behind the counter and aimed a single bark at the closed door.

"That's telling her, Bear," Mary said, laughing.

"Don't tease him," Kaylee said. "I don't blame him for finding Roz a little intimidating."

Though the shop was definitely far from swamped for the rest of the morning, they did have a handful of browsers, more than they'd seen recently. By midmorning, Kaylee had to slip back to the work area to put together some more small arrangements while Mary chatted with customers.

As she worked, Bear lagged behind on the sales floor, enjoying the attention of the newcomers, but he finally joined her, flopping down at her feet.

"All that socializing wore you out, huh?" Kaylee asked as she slipped a sprig of baby's breath into the short vase in front of her. It also held a single golden rosebud whose petals were tipped in red. The rose had arrived with a broken stem, making it no good for larger arrangements, but the bloom was the perfect focal point of this small bouquet.

While she worked, Kaylee couldn't keep nagging questions about Jeanette from distracting her. She was sure her lack of sleep wasn't helping, but mostly she felt an increasing pressure boiling in her. What could have made Jeanette think she should abandon everything and fake her own death?

When the little arrangement was finished, Kaylee carried it out to the front cooler. The browsers had come and gone, and she figured it was a good time to head over to the inn and see if she could catch Margaret Olber.

Mary agreed to the idea immediately. "It'll do you good to get some fresh air," she said.

Kaylee glanced toward the window. The air had been a little too fresh and cold lately for her taste, but she had to admit that it would probably help wake her up. "Do you mind if I leave Bear?" she asked. "The inn has a cat now, and I don't need the distraction of a cat versus dog showdown."

Surprise colored Mary's face. "Since when do they have a cat?"

"Apparently the poor thing was abandoned by a guest," Kaylee said.

Mary frowned. "What is wrong with people? Don't they realize pet ownership is a commitment?"

Kaylee raised her hands. "No argument here. I can't imagine a scenario in which I would leave Bear behind and never come back. Though the cat does seem to be a handful. Its behavior while I was there was very erratic."

"No one actually understands cats," Mary said. "Their air of mystery is part of their appeal." She and Herb had recently adopted a sweet calico named Lily, and the kitty had brought much joy into their house.

"I suppose." Kaylee put on her coat and wrapped her neck in a soft knit scarf she'd gotten from her grandmother for Christmas. Then she opened the door to the chill and headed for the inn. She could have driven, of course, but since rain wasn't in the forecast for the day, she hated to duck out of the walk simply because it was going to be cold. Thinking like that would have her horribly out of shape by spring.

As she walked by shops and down mostly empty sidewalks, the peacefulness of Turtle Cove in winter worked its magic on her. She noticed how charming the little town was as if for the first time. The sidewalk climbed steadily up a small hill toward the inn, making Kaylee's calves ache. But then she reached a spot that opened up a view toward the marina. The breeze whipped the water into small white peaks and made the moored boats bob. Not far from the port, a bald eagle swooped down over the water in search of a meal.

In the summer, the same view would include sailboats and kayaks, but the rougher waters of Puget Sound in winter didn't invite that kind of activity. Without the bright dots of color from such craft, the sound appeared wilder, more the way Kaylee imagined the first inhabitants must have seen it.

A blast of cold air ruffled her hair and urged her the rest of the way to the inn. She hustled into the old building and paused, letting the warmth soak into her. She expected to see Stella, but a different woman stood behind the front desk. This one was vaguely familiar, though Kaylee couldn't place her.

"Kaylee Bleu," the woman said. "Surely you don't need a room?"

"Thankfully no." Kaylee walked close enough to see the woman's name tag. *Rachel. Do I know a Rachel?*

The woman must have noticed Kaylee's glance at her name tag. "I've come into The Flower Patch once or twice. I love your arrangements, but cut flowers always make me sad when they die."

"We also sell flowering houseplants," Kaylee said. "And dried flower arrangements can be nice too."

The woman relented. "I hadn't considered that. I'll come by and pick something up."

"You're always welcome." Kaylee spotted Lucky sprawled in a chair nearby. The cat blinked at her sleepily. *She seems calm enough now.* She returned her attention to Rachel. "I actually came in to chat with Margaret Olber. Is she in her room?"

"Nope." Rachel grinned and lowered her voice, nodding

toward the stairs. "She's right there."

When Kaylee made eye contact, Margaret waved and asked hopefully, "Are you here to see me?"

"I am," Kaylee said. "I thought we might have a chat about Jeanette."

Margaret glanced toward the sleeping cat and shuddered. "We can talk in the library. This inn has the most amazing collection of nautical books."

The inn's library was news to Kaylee, so she followed Margaret with interest. The small room was tucked behind the stairs. The decor inside resembled the rest of the inn, with blue-and-white wallpaper above weathered wainscoting. Several floor-to-ceiling bookcases in the same worn wood lined the walls, and overstuffed chairs upholstered in navy blue were scattered throughout.

After closing the library door carefully, Margaret settled into one of the chairs and gestured for Kaylee to sit in another. "Have you decided to include me in the investigation?"

Kaylee skirted the question. "I was hoping you could give me some information. Someone suggested to me that Jeanette might have been in a relationship with someone other than her ex-husband, maybe someone at work. Had you heard anything about that?"

Margaret blinked in surprise, then pressed her lips together and seemed to think about it. Finally, she shook her head. "Not a thing, and you know how gossipy offices can be. I don't have the foggiest idea how she'd hide that. She did work closely with one man, Stew Lascar, and they always seemed friendly enough. No more than that, though."

"You don't think they could have hidden a romance?" Kaylee asked.

"I don't think so. Maybe." Margaret's expression conveyed mild distress. "I don't want to give the idea that we do nothing in the office but gossip. It's not like that. Most people there *do* mind their own business, but there are always a few."

Kaylee thought of her own days working as a plant taxonomy professor at the University of Washington. The people she'd worked with were always poking into each other's business. The gossip had been constant, and though Kaylee tried hard not to participate, it was hard to avoid. "So Jeanette never dated openly at work?"

"Well, not for a long time," Margaret said. "About two years ago she did date one of the upper managers, Devon Herbert. I don't think it ever amounted to much. I never understood the attraction, personally. He always seemed rather dour to me, and Jeanette was anything but that."

Kaylee decided to mention both Stew Lascar and Devon Herbert to Nick. He would certainly be able to follow up on them more easily than Kaylee could. She'd also need to tell him about Bart's jealous side. "Did Jeanette ever mention being afraid of her ex?"

Again Margaret seemed surprised. "Jeanette never mentioned being afraid of anyone. I'd have trouble imagining it. She wasn't the fearful sort. She did mention her ex once or twice, but she seemed to think him a rather silly man."

As if conjured up by their conversation, the door to the library opened and Bart walked in, a thick book in one hand. He did a double take at the sight of Kaylee and Margaret in the chairs, then he pushed the door mostly closed and walked over with a wide smile on his face.

"Ms. Bleu," he said. "I wanted to thank you for the other day. The news of Jeanette's death came as a terrible shock. I was struggling and you were kind."

"I'm glad I could help," Kaylee said. "Have you met Margaret?"

Kaylee watched his face closely, but from the curious glances he gave Margaret, he'd never met her. "I don't believe so. Do you work here at the inn?"

Margaret laughed. "Hardly. I worked with Jeanette on the mainland."

"I never had the opportunity to meet anyone from Jeanette's office." An air of deep sadness radiated from Bart. "I was Jeanette's husband." He sighed deeply. "Actually, ex-husband, though I hate that phrase. But at any rate, I believe Jeanette enjoyed her work."

Kaylee observed him with interest. *Apparently Jeanette talked about her work differently to him than she did to Roz. Unless he was simply being kind.*

"She was good at it," Margaret said.

Not wanting to seem insensitive to Margaret and Bart's grief, Kaylee was at a bit of a loss for what to say. Her attention shifted between them for any sign of anger or animosity, but she saw only shared sadness.

A faint squeak drew Kaylee's attention to the doorway, and she saw Lucky push the cracked door open just enough to slip through. The cat rushed across the room and immediately tried to climb into Margaret's purse.

The woman snatched up the bag and hugged it against her as she jumped to her feet. "Shoo! Go away! Why does that awful cat keep bothering me?"

Bart bent and scooped up the cat. He held Lucky firmly, but the cat's gaze never wavered from the purse. "I don't think it meant any harm," Bart said. "Have you carried any food in your bag? It could be the cat is simply after a snack."

"Perhaps it's a lingering scent from the to-go box you had in there the other night," Kaylee suggested.

"What is the horrible little beast after?" Margaret backed up another few paces. "I never cared for cats. In fact, I'm a little bit phobic." Keeping her narrow-eyed gaze on Lucky, she gave

Bart and the cat a wide berth as she headed for the door. "If you don't mind, I think I'll go try to rest. I find this very upsetting." She practically ran from the room.

"Do you hear that?" Bart asked the cat. "You scared the poor woman. I hope you're ashamed of yourself." Lucky watched the door for another few seconds, then succumbed to Bart's petting and purred loudly. "I've always enjoyed cats, but they're ridiculous sometimes. I had a cat when I was a kid, and my father loathed it, so the cat was constantly jumping into his lap. I think they do that sort of thing just to push buttons."

Kaylee reached out to rub Lucky's ears. "Well if that's the case here, you're a very naughty cat."

If Lucky was disturbed by the gentle scolding, she showed no sign and merely purred louder. Bart scratched the cat under the chin and cooed at her, making it harder and harder for Kaylee to imagine him killing anyone. Of all the people connected with Jeanette, only one had shown a dangerous side — and it wasn't the man cuddling the abandoned cat.

15

The breeze at Kaylee's back picked up as she walked to The Flower Patch, almost as if it were hurrying her to work. When it blew her through the flower shop door, Bear greeted her with all the enthusiasm that could fit in such a small dog.

"He is adorable."

Kaylee glanced up from petting Bear to the two smiling women standing at the front counter. One of the women wore a coat so puffy she resembled an inflatable raft, while the other sported little more than a twill jacket against the chill outside. Kaylee recognized both women from church, though she wasn't sure she'd seen either in the shop before. "Thank you."

"Oh, is he yours?" the woman in the puffy coat asked. "That's right. I heard you had a little dog. He's so friendly."

"Dachshunds can be cranky sometimes," her friend added.

"I don't think Bear has a cranky bone in his body." Kaylee walked around the counter to stand beside Mary, and Bear followed her. "Did you ladies find what you needed?"

"Oh yes," the puffy coat lady said. "I love this soap." She snatched up a bar. "DeeDee Wilcox makes it, isn't that right?"

"She does," Kaylee confirmed.

"I've only talked to her at church, but she seems like a lovely person," the woman said with a smile.

The twill-jacketed woman leaned closer to the counter and whispered, "Were you out sleuthing?"

Kaylee drew back in surprise. "Excuse me?"

"Oh, you don't have to pretend with us," the puffy coat lady said. "We've heard all about you."

"And how you're trying to prove Roz Corzo didn't kill that woman," her friend added. "We both think that it's very charitable of you to help her out. She's *so* rude."

Kaylee reflected that the women apparently didn't consider busybody behavior to be rude, but she decided not to comment on it. Instead, she simply smiled. "I'm sure the Orcas Island Sheriff's Department has the investigation well in hand." She gestured toward the bar of soap in the woman's hand. "Is that all for today?"

Both women frowned in unison and the puffy-coated woman dropped the soap back into the display. "Actually, I don't think we need anything today after all." They marched out of the shop, but Kaylee heard the word "rude" drift in on the wind as the door closed behind them.

Mary burst into laughter. "You'd better steel yourself. Apparently the word is out. Those two aren't the first who've been in trying to get information."

Kaylee harrumphed. "I hope the others bought something."

"Actually they did," Mary said. "We're nearly out of arrangements in the cooler again, so you might want to make some more." Her grin returned. "Especially since I think I see some more mystery enthusiasts heading toward the door."

Kaylee hurried to the work area with Bear at her heels. Once out of sight, Kaylee pulled out her phone and called Nick. "I have some information about Jeanette," she said in greeting.

Nick groaned. "Is this you leaving the whole thing alone? Why do I even bother saying that to you anymore?"

"Beats me. Roz said Bart's jealousy is part of what broke him and Jeanette up in the first place. So I asked Margaret Olber if Jeanette was interested in anyone at work."

"Kaylee," Nick said with the exaggerated patience he used when he thought she was wrong. "Pop Ronson has admitted to taking money from Jeanette to get her off Roz's boat. Don't you think it's much more reasonable to think something went wrong during that process and he is lying to cover it up?"

"Reese doesn't think so," Kaylee said. "He said he can't see Pop being so heartless to Jeanette's family, and I trust Reese's judgment."

"I'll admit his judgment in some things certainly seems sound."

Something in Nick's tone made Kaylee suspicious. "Like what?"

"Never mind. What did Margaret have to say about Jeanette's love life?"

Kaylee still wondered what Nick had meant about Reese, but she filed it away as something to pry into at a later time. "She said she didn't know of anyone Jeanette was actively involved with, but she did work closely with a man named Stew Lascar. Margaret had no idea if it went beyond work, but they were together a lot."

"That seems a little weak," Nick grumbled.

"You still might want to talk to him. Also, apparently Jeanette dated a man named Devon Herbert about two years ago. Margaret hadn't heard of any recent romance between them, but it wasn't impossible. You might want to talk to him too."

"I'm sorry, but neither of those sounds particularly likely."

"It's all right. I'm sure Margaret can get me their phone numbers," Kaylee said innocently. "I'd be happy to look into it and tell you if I come up with anything."

"You will do no such thing. *I'll* call and see what those two have to say, but I'm not expecting anything to come of it. I still think this is going to turn out to be Pop, whether accidental or intentional."

"And I think it won't."

"Guess we'll find out which of us is right," Nick said, then his tone changed. "Kaylee, I went out to your place yesterday to try to get some measurements of that shoe print Reese spotted, but the rain had washed it away. I'm sorry."

"That's okay," Kaylee said. "I still think it was an innocent passerby."

"Maybe you ought to ask your neighbors," Nick said. "You know, dig into something that's actually your business for once."

"Maybe I will," Kaylee said, miffed that Nick wasn't taking her ideas seriously.

To her surprise, Nick had another question. "This interest in Jeanette's coworkers presupposes her ex is a violent guy. What do you think of him?"

"I thought you were unimpressed with my opinions," Kaylee said.

"Not your opinions about people. I can't base an investigation on them, but I'm always open to hearing what you think."

Kaylee sat on one of the stools in the design area, suddenly tired of the whole situation. "Honestly, Nick, I think he's a nice guy. He seems truly heartbroken over Jeanette. But I've misjudged people before."

"Haven't we all," Nick said. "All right, I'll make the calls to the mainland. In exchange, I do think you ought to chat with your neighbors. Reese and I would both feel better if we knew who'd been walking around on your property in the dark."

"Fine," Kaylee said. "I'll ask."

But after she hung up with Nick, she didn't immediately make the calls. Instead, she focused on creating some new flower arrangements for the front cooler. From her spot in the workroom, she could hear Mary's conversation with the steady flow of customers coming in. Kaylee would have been heartened at so much business if it weren't for the patrons' questions about her and the investigation into Jeanette's death that floated back to her.

"I'm thinking we're going to hide back here for a long time," she whispered to Bear.

He merely blinked at her before settling down as if he understood.

Kaylee contemplated the cluster of small bouquets. She was going to have to be brave and carry them out to the cooler, even if it meant deflecting questions about Jeanette.

Mary came in, startling Kaylee into dropping a carnation.

"Oh, sorry," Mary said as Kaylee picked up the flower and examined it for possible bruising. "I wanted to tell you that the coast is clear for now. I'll help you carry out these arrangements. The front coolers are pretty picked over."

Kaylee trailed along behind Mary, her hands full of vases. "It's silly to hide from customers, isn't it?"

"The problem is that if they see you, they're going to want you to answer their questions," Mary said as they walked to the cooler. "And if you don't..." She nodded toward the soap display where the annoyed woman had dropped her near-purchase.

"I get it." Kaylee pulled open the cooler door and loaded in the flowers from her hands. "At least we have business. Has everyone asked about Jeanette?"

Mary offered a wry smile. "Pretty much. The ones who didn't ask about Jeanette all asked about you, so I'm thinking they would have asked about Jeanette if you'd been handy."

"How did I get to be the center of this?" Kaylee asked.

Mary handed her an arrangement. "First of all, you seem to end up in the center of every unusual occurrence in Turtle Cove. And this time, you have Roz as well."

"Roz!" Kaylee froze with the vase in her hand. "I can't exactly see Roz being that social."

"No, but someone probably gossiped about Roz right in front of her, maybe at the grocery store. And if they mentioned the whole drinking thing, there's no way Roz would let that go without comment."

"You're right about that," Kaylee said. "But how would I come into it?"

"I think Roz is hoping you'll be her character witness," Mary said. "Her proof that she's not guilty. If Kaylee Bleu is working to clear her name, then Roz must be innocent."

Kaylee groaned. "That's a little convoluted."

Mary closed the cooler. "So is gossip."

The front door opened and both women froze in alarm. Jessica took one look at their faces and asked, "What? What happened now?"

Mary and Kaylee exchanged a glance, then laughed for far longer than the humor of the situation warranted, making Kaylee realize how stressed she'd been. Jessica waited with her hands on her hips for them to regain control.

Finally, Kaylee managed to say, "Sorry, Jess. We've been under siege all day from people wanting to gossip about Jeanette. I've been hiding from them, and I thought I'd been caught."

"Not by me," Jessica said. "I came in to get a bouquet for my dining room table with no ulterior motives. Though I should tell you Oliver's leaves are curling. I think he's stressed about something, like a potential threat."

"I'll keep that in mind." Kaylee stepped away from the cooler. "As it happens, we have a nice selection of arrangements."

Jessica surveyed the packed cooler and giggled. "I think I can guess where you were hiding."

After Jessica left, Kaylee and Mary hung an out-to-lunch sign on the door and headed to the kitchen for sandwiches and a chance to relax. Kaylee caught Mary up on her chat with Nick while they ate.

"He has a point," Mary said in reply. "You should ask your neighbors about the print."

Kaylee tucked a bit of fallen lettuce into her sandwich. "I guess I'm afraid no one will admit to having taken a walk on my land. Then all I can do is worry about intruders, and I'm not sleeping that great already."

Kaylee took a bite, then nearly choked on it in surprise when Mary said, "Maybe you ought to marry Reese so you have someone around to keep you safe."

After chewing furiously and taking a drink of water, Kaylee said, "That's not funny. I almost choked. Poor Reese isn't a punch line."

Mary chuckled. "He might be amused by the expression on your face right now. Though, I *do* think he'd be perfect for you, and I would worry less if you had a big, strong man around to watch out for you." She said the words lightly, but there was honest concern beneath them.

"I have Bear."

Bear perked up at the sound of his name, and Kaylee snuck him a scrap of cheese as a sign of solidarity.

"And Bear is wonderful," Mary agreed, "but he's not exactly an attack dog."

"What happened to our relaxing lunch? Tell me about your garden. Do you have any updates planned in the spring?"

Though Mary raised an eyebrow at Kaylee's change of subject, she went along with it cheerfully enough. Mary loved talking about her garden.

The rest of the day passed with fewer customers. Apparently word had gotten around that The Flower Patch was not a good source of gossip, and eventually Kaylee stopped hiding in the workroom. As annoying as the gossipers had been, Kaylee had to admit it was probably their most profitable day since Valentine's Day.

As the afternoon shadows became full darkness pressing against the shop windows, Kaylee told Mary to go home. "You went above and beyond today. Go put your feet up."

Mary scanned the shop. "I should sweep, and we need to take out the trash."

"I can do both of those. Go." Kaylee flapped a hand at her.

Mary conceded and gathered her belongings. "Lock the door after me," she directed.

"I will, worrywart."

Mary smiled but still issued a warning. "And be careful on the way home."

Kaylee drew on her chest with her finger. "Cross my heart."

Once Mary left, Kaylee gave Bear a treat and promised they'd leave in a few minutes. "You seem to be as ready to go home as I am."

Kaylee quickly swept the front room, then spot-cleaned fingerprints off glass shelves with a soft rag. Once that was complete, all she had to do was take out the trash and they could get on the road.

"I'll be right back," she said to Bear as she hauled the bag out the back door. She'd barely gotten down the steps before Bear started barking wildly from the doorway.

Kaylee froze. A man stepped out of the shadows and into the pool of light cast by the security light. She immediately recognized Lyle Colson and her entire body tensed. She gripped the trash bag tightly, wondering if she'd be able to use it to defend herself. "What do you want, Mr. Colson?"

He shoved his hands into his pockets and shifted from foot to foot. "I want to know what really happened to my sister."

"And you think I can tell you?"

"I think you can give me more information than I have," he said.

Kaylee watched him uneasily. How would he react when she didn't give him the answers he clearly wanted? She glanced toward

Death by Chocolate. If she screamed, would Jessica hear her?

"I honestly have no idea," Kaylee said.

Lyle stared at her, his expression blank, and Kaylee waited for the inevitable explosion. Instead, the big man's face crumpled. "I have to find out," he said hoarsely. "I have to find her killer."

"You loved your sister that much?" Kaylee asked, trying not to sound as doubtful as she felt.

He hung his head. "No. Not really. I was so mad at her."

"Why?"

His eyes narrowed. "My parents never saw her for the selfish, conniving person she was. Never. They thought she was perfect. She was all they talked about. She was all they saw."

"That had to be hard," Kaylee said.

"It doesn't matter." He held her gaze, not bothering to swipe at the tears running down his face. "My parents are old now. Dad's almost ninety. I can do this one thing. I can find out who killed Jeanette. It'll matter. If I do it, it'll matter to them."

What could she say? The man's open pain hurt her heart, but it didn't exactly make him seem innocent. In fact, it just gave him another reason to want Jeanette out of the picture.

Lyle took a step toward Kaylee, his hand held out, but she never found out what he was going to say.

"Hold it right there, Mr. Colson," Nick said sternly, stepping out of the darkness. "What do you think you're doing, accosting Ms. Bleu in the dark?"

Lyle's gaze darted around before settling on Kaylee. "I only wanted to talk to her."

"That's what phones are for, Mr. Colson," Nick said. "I think you'd better come with me. We can talk."

The big man perked up at that. "About Jeanette? Did you find something out?"

"I found out her brother is acting very strangely."

Shadows clouded Lyle's face. "You better not be planning to pin Jeanette's murder on me."

"I don't pin crimes on people," Nick said. "I investigate, and I ask questions. And right now, I have questions for you." He peered at Kaylee. "Are you okay?"

"I'm fine," Kaylee said, though she still felt more than a little shaken from the encounter. "We were simply talking."

Nick nodded and led the other man away. Kaylee watched them. She couldn't help but be touched by Lyle Colson's pain, but people in pain could do terrible things sometimes. She shivered in the cold. *Is that what happened to Jeanette?*

16

Kaylee expected to experience another rough night of sleep, but after she had a light supper and spent some time cuddling on the sofa with Bear, she found that falling asleep came easily on Friday night. On Saturday morning, she actually hummed while she tugged Bear's little jacket on to him. When she realized she was doing it, she stopped in surprise.

"Wow, a good night's sleep seems to have helped my mood." Bear wagged his tail and Kaylee patted him on the head. Then she groaned. "I hope today isn't another parade of gossips through the store." Bear gave her a consoling lick and she laughed. "Right. You don't mind as long as they make a fuss over you."

As Kaylee pulled on her coat, the phone in her pocket rang. She fished it out and saw it was Nick calling. "Good morning, Deputy Durham."

"You sound chipper this morning."

"Weird, isn't it? I even slept well." Kaylee tucked the phone against her shoulder so she could do up the fasteners on her coat.

"I hate to do anything that dampens that good mood, but I wanted to update you since you've ended up involved in this despite my best efforts."

Kaylee shifted the phone to her hand, and reached out with the other hand for Bear's leash. "Oh, please, you were perfectly happy to accept my involvement when you needed those tea dregs analyzed."

"The problem is that once you're in an investigation, you tend to be all in." Nick's tone was more teasing than accusatory, which Kaylee took to mean he didn't entirely mind her meddling.

"I thought you were going to update me," she said in her sweetest tone as she knelt to snap the leash on Bear.

"We're holding Lyle Colson under suspicion," Nick said. "He had a small vial in his jacket pocket, and I'm thinking it's ground valerian root. Could you tell by looking at it, or do you need a microscope?"

"I should see it under a microscope to be totally certain," she said, scooping up Bear to keep him from dancing around her feet while he waited for her to open the door. "What did Lyle say about it?"

"He insists that he doesn't know how it got there and is presently bellowing that I planted it on him," Nick said. "It's amazing how often evidence simply appears in the possession of suspects. It's enough to make a guy believe in magic."

"If it is valerian in the vial, that would mean he almost certainly had contact with his sister after she knocked Roz out."

"That's what I figured as well. And that isn't all."

Kaylee tucked the phone against her shoulder again to free a hand to open the door. "What else?"

"We searched his room at the inn and found a piece of a woman's scarf stuffed in the pocket of a pair of dirty jeans. Jeanette's body wasn't wearing a scarf when it was found, but she had been in the water for a while."

Kaylee set Bear on the ground outside and closed her eyes, thinking back to when she saw Jeanette and Roz at Jessica's shop. She remembered Jeanette had been wearing a lovely wool coat and a floral scarf. She described the scarf to Nick.

"Sounds like a match to the piece we found," Nick said. "I'll show it to you when you come in to examine the contents of the vial. Any chance you could do it today?"

"Probably," Kaylee said. "I've got to talk to Mary though, and I'm not at the shop yet. In fact, I'm not out of my front yard.

I'll have to call you back when I'm sure she can watch the shop while I'm upstairs."

"That'll be fine," Nick said. "And thanks, by the way."

"Thanks?" Kaylee echoed.

"For not saying 'I told you so' about Roz and Pop. Apparently neither one was the culprit."

"Apparently." Kaylee kept her tone vague, but the whole situation still bothered her. Could Lyle have killed his sister? Or could it have been an accident as she had suspected of Pop? She barely noticed when Nick said goodbye. In fact, she didn't realize she hadn't been moving until Bear began pulling at the leash, clearly eager to get to the car and out of the cold.

"You're right, Bear," Kaylee said. "Time to get the day going."

When she arrived at The Flower Patch, she couldn't park and get inside fast enough. The warmth of the shop was a welcome relief from the chill.

"I think it's gotten colder out," Kaylee told Mary as she removed her coat as well as Bear's.

"It may dissuade some of our gossip traffic," Mary said. "Unfortunately, it may dissuade all of our traffic."

"Possibly." Kaylee hung up the outerwear, then turned back to Mary. "I talked to Nick this morning. They're holding Lyle Colson."

"When did they arrest him?"

"Last night, when he was yelling at me behind our shop."

Mary gasped. "Behind the shop! I knew I shouldn't have left you alone. Are you all right?"

"I'm fine. He never touched me," Kaylee said. "But Nick says they've found some evidence to tie him to Jeanette's disappearance. He wants me to examine a vial that might have ground valerian root in it."

"I'm glad they're finally making headway on the case," Mary said. "I was starting to worry. Whenever you need your scientist time, take it. I'll fend off the hordes of customers."

"I'll give Nick a call and let him set the time since you're flexible," Kaylee said. Just as she pulled out her phone, however, it rang.

"Good morning!" DeeDee sang out when Kaylee answered. "Your book came in and is ready to go to its new home."

"Great," Kaylee said. "That will give me some interesting reading for the weekend. I'll swing by later today."

DeeDee chuckled. "I love gardening, but an academic text on toxic plants isn't exactly something I'd curl up with over the weekend."

"We all have our passions," Kaylee said with a laugh. "But I am mostly interested in it to help with the work I do for the sheriff's department."

"Sure, sure," DeeDee teased. "I remember. But don't be surprised if I don't buy the next thing you make for a church bake sale."

"I'll remember that."

After she finished with DeeDee, she called Nick and set a time in the late morning for him to come by The Flower Patch with the vial of plant matter. Once she was done with phone calls, she committed to focusing on the flower shop and putting thoughts of Jeanette's death completely out of her head. The morning's customer traffic didn't compare with the day before, but they did have a few shoppers and most actually seemed more interested in flowers than gossip. Kaylee started to hope the island was going back to normal.

During a lull, Kaylee clipped a leash on Bear. "I'm going to take Bear for a quick walk and pick up the book from DeeDee if you don't mind."

"Have a nice walk," Mary said. "It makes me chilly to think about it."

As she'd expected, it was uncomfortably cold out, but Kaylee turned up her coat collar and tried to be grateful. *At least it's not raining*. If Bear found the day unpleasant, he showed no sign as he trotted along cheerfully, pausing only to give various objects a thorough sniffing.

After walking until Kaylee was starting to shiver, they crossed the street and started back on the other side so they could go to the bookshop. Kaylee noticed that even Bear seemed eager to enter the store, pulling at the leash and pressing his nose against the glass door.

Inside Between the Lines, warmth seeped slowly into Kaylee and she gratefully shucked off her coat, intending to stay until she stopped shivering. To her surprise, she spotted the cat from the Northern Lights Inn sprawled on the counter.

Bear rushed closer in what was probably intended to be a friendly greeting. Unimpressed, Lucky merely gazed languidly down at the little dog. Kaylee rubbed the cat's head. "I've met this kitty," she said to DeeDee, who stood at the register. "She was at the inn."

DeeDee nodded. "I got a panicky call about her. Apparently she kept harassing a guest, so I agreed to a temporary visit—emphasis on temporary. I am not interested in a shop cat."

"I'm going to hazard a guess that the harassed guest was Margaret Olber, Jeanette Colson's former coworker." Kaylee stroked the cat's soft fur. "I'm surprised at how relaxed and calm she seems considering how hyper I've seen her around Margaret."

"Cats are strange," DeeDee said. "I had one years ago who was transfixed by invisible things. He would stare into space intently until it creeped me out, then wander off and find a new spot to do the same thing again. He had me convinced my house was haunted."

Lucky stood up and stretched, then jumped down to sniff noses with Bear. Bear wagged his tail enthusiastically and turned puppy dog eyes on Kaylee.

"Don't get any ideas," she said. "We do not need a kitty

roommate." The cat purred loudly and rubbed against Kaylee's leg. "Sorry, Lucky, but I have years of practice standing up to cuteness."

"Sure." DeeDee chuckled. "Because you're such a stern disciplinarian with Bear."

"It comes and goes," Kaylee admitted, joining in DeeDee's laughter. While they were giggling together, Andy pushed open the door, letting Zoe and Polly precede him into the shop.

"It's freezing out there!" Zoe complained, then her face brightened. "Bear!" She ran across the room and dropped to her knees to pet Bear with one hand and Lucky with the other.

The cat crawled up into the girl's lap, purring loudly all the while. Kaylee wondered again how the hyper cat from the inn had transformed into the sweet creature that snuggled with Zoe.

Bear watched Zoe and the cat, and nudged the cat with his nose. Kaylee chuckled. Bear clearly wasn't sure he wanted to share his playmate, but then Polly plopped down on the floor next to Bear and began rubbing his ears.

"We're starting to resemble a pet shop," Andy said.

"I won't be leaving Bear here this time," Kaylee said, eliciting a disappointed groan from Polly. "I only came to pick up a book."

"And here it is." DeeDee handed it over. "Honestly, I'm a little surprised at how thick it is. I knew there were toxic plants, of course, but this is a whopper."

"It covers plants from all over the world," Kaylee said. "Including some that aren't particularly toxic until you concentrate the chemicals in them."

"Aren't you full of terrifying information," Andy said. "If you were married, I might call and warn your husband."

Kaylee cheerfully went along with the teasing. "If I ever get married, I'll make sure it's to someone who doesn't need poisoning."

She chatted with her friends for another few minutes to give Bear time to enjoy the girls. Finally he disentangled himself from

Polly's affection and peered up expectantly at Kaylee, clearly ready to leave.

"I'd better get to the shop," Kaylee said. "Nick is stopping by in a bit on department business."

"Bear can stay here," Zoe volunteered, scrambling to her feet with the cat in her arms.

"Not today," her mom said firmly. "One animal is the Between the Lines limit."

Zoe pouted for a couple seconds before the cat bumped her chin with her head, and Zoe completely forgot to sulk. Instead she started off for the storage room, murmuring to the cat, "I have such a nice hat for you."

Andy laughed heartily. "Now that's a patient cat."

"You wouldn't say that if you'd seen her at the inn," Kaylee said.

Andy shrugged. "Fair enough. No one can predict a cat's behavior. They do what they do, and humans try to keep up."

"You're probably right," Kaylee agreed, then wished them all a good day and put on her coat and headed out into the cold. After warming up at Between the Lines, she walked briskly to the flower shop and managed to get inside before she started shivering again.

As she hurried in, she spotted Nick leaning on the counter, his face grim. Kaylee felt a rush of alarm. "What is it? What's happened now?"

17

Mary took one look at Kaylee and waved her hands dismissively. "Nothing's happened. I was telling Nick a sad story from my days as a dispatcher."

Kaylee's shoulders sagged with relief. "I guess I've had a stressful last few days. Sorry I overreacted." She walked behind the counter and sank down on the stool, placing the book she'd bought beside the cash register. Bear didn't even tug on the leash to pause for a petting from his favorite deputy, sticking by Kaylee's side instead.

"I came by to see if we could move up our appointment," Nick said. "I had to schedule some witness statements in the time we originally planned on. So I thought I'd swing by and see if you could examine the vial now."

"Sure," Kaylee said. "If Mary doesn't mind my disappearing upstairs right after I got back."

"That would be fine. Bear and I enjoy each other's company thoroughly," Mary said. As if to prove her willingness, she gently took the leash from Kaylee and bent to unsnap it from Bear's collar.

"While you still have your coat on, can you go next door with me?" Nick asked Kaylee. "I brought along the piece of scarf, and I'd appreciate it if you and Jessica took a look since you both saw Jeanette." Then Nick grinned. "And if we happen to get some of her amazing coffee to go, that would be fine too."

Kaylee returned the smile. "I'm up for that."

Jessica's shop was empty when they walked in, a rare event even in the cold months, and Jessica greeted them warmly. "Let me guess," she said. "Hot chocolate?"

Kaylee had been intending to have coffee, but at Jessica's words, she realized how much nicer cocoa would be. "Yes, please."

"Coffee for me," Nick said. "And information."

Jessica began fixing the drinks immediately. "Information?"

Nick pulled an evidence bag from his inner jacket pocket. "Do you recognize this scarf?"

Jessica leaned across the counter and studied it closely. "Whose is it?"

"I was hoping you could tell me."

Jessica sighed and shrugged. "I'm not sure. I get a lot of customers." Then her eyes widened. "The dead lady. You think it belongs to her, right? She was wearing a scarf, I remember that."

"Was it this one?" Nick asked.

"Maybe." Jessica's voice trailed off and she glanced at Kaylee. "What do you think?"

"It could be the scarf I remember," Kaylee said hesitantly. "But it's hard to tell. It's only a piece, and it's filthy."

"Thanks, ladies," Nick said. "I'll show it to Roz. She saw more of Jeanette. She might remember better."

Jessica laughed. "Right, I'm sure Roz noticed a scarf."

Nick shrugged. "We can always hope."

Nick paid for the two hot beverages, and Kaylee followed him outside after saying goodbye to Jessica.

As they returned to The Flower Patch and went up to Kaylee's makeshift lab, Nick said, "I'm sorry we scared you earlier."

"It's not your fault," Kaylee said. "Honestly, I don't know what my problem is. I woke up so happy this morning, but I've been discombobulated lately." Then she poked him lightly as they started up the stairs. "And it didn't help for you and Reese to worry me half to death about the footprints in my yard."

"Did you call your neighbors?"

"Not yet." She rolled her eyes. "And you're doing it again.

It's no wonder I'm ready to jump out of my skin."

"I'm pretty sure we've got the right guy in custody," Nick said. "You can relax."

"He's certainly angry enough," Kaylee hedged as she unlocked and opened the door to her lab.

Nick followed her into the room. "I think there's something he's not telling us. The sheriff is questioning him, and my guess is that Colson is going to crack soon. Once he does, we can close the door on the whole thing."

"Hopefully," Kaylee said, flicking on the bright overhead lights.

Kaylee put on gloves and Nick shook the vial out of an evidence bag into her hands. She held it up to the light.

"At a glance, I'd say it's some kind of ground root," she said. "Now to make sure it's valerian and not ginger or something similar." Even as she said it, she knew the material in the vial wasn't ginger or anything else. But she had to be positive. She prepared a tiny bit of the ground material on a slide.

Within moments, she was sure. "This is definitely valerian. It's identical to the material in the tea Roz drank."

"Only less wet," Nick said.

"Yes." She picked up the vial and held it out to him. He opened the evidence bag and let her drop it in. Then he held up a finger and fished his phone out of his jacket pocket, stepping away to answer it.

Kaylee busied herself with cleaning up the work area while she waited for Nick to finish. When he finally walked over, his expression was serious. "It's settled."

Kaylee froze. "Lyle confessed."

"No. He still says he has no idea how the vial got into his pocket and no idea how a piece of Jeanette's scarf ended up in his jeans, but he did tell the sheriff why he was so angry with his sister recently."

"Something other than jealousy?" Kaylee asked.

"Other, though possibly related. According to Lyle, Jeanette called him and admitted to embezzling money from her employers. In fact, apparently she'd gloated about it, saying she would be rich and Lyle would always barely scrape by and grovel to get their parents' approval."

"Wow," Kaylee said. "That's harsh."

Nick nodded. "Harsh, and a prime motive. The sheriff said Colson was in a rage simply talking about what an embarrassment that was going to be to his parents."

"Did the sheriff confirm the embezzling?" Kaylee asked.

"Not yet. The company is closed for the weekend. We'll have to wait until Monday to get someone to confirm."

"You could ask Margaret Olber," Kaylee suggested. "I'm sure she's still at the inn."

Nick looked at Kaylee in surprise. "I'd have thought she would be gone by now."

"She was at the inn yesterday."

"Thanks. I'll definitely have a chat with her. If she can confirm the crime, we'll have this pretty much sewn up."

"Though Lyle still says he didn't do it," Kaylee reminded him.

Nick snorted. "They all say that."

The rest of the day passed with a smattering of customers, most coming to The Flower Patch for specific items rather than simply browsing. Kaylee couldn't quite sort out why she felt restless. The sheriff's department was convinced they'd found Jeanette's killer, even if they did have some details to sort out, and Kaylee had to admit, Lyle had been a scary guy. *Surely I should feel better now?*

"Maybe today should be your day to slip out early," Mary suggested. "You could do something fun tonight and get your mind off how strange things have been."

Kaylee picked up the book she'd gotten from DeeDee's shop. "I suppose I could do some reading."

Mary snatched it from her. "No scary books. You need something cheerful. How about a nice romance novel? I think Bea had some upstairs somewhere."

"Grandma read romance novels?" Kaylee's eyes widened in shock.

"When she wanted to relax. Do you want me to run up and see if I can find one?" Before Kaylee could answer, the door opened and Reese walked in. Mary's grin became mischievous and she whispered, "Never mind. The real thing has come in."

Kaylee gave her a warning glance before focusing on Reese. "Shopping for flowers?"

His expression grew sheepish. "Not today. That's twice now." He surveyed. "Maybe I should get some. They'd brighten up my cabin."

"Don't worry about that," Mary said. "You're welcome to come by anytime to chat. It can get lonely around here in the cold months." She gave Kaylee a pointed glance, and Kaylee frowned back.

"I know what you mean," Reese said, not seeming to catch any undercurrent between the two women. "I was going over to O'Brien's for supper, and the thought of eating alone is depressing this time of year. I thought I'd see if you'd care to join me, Kaylee." Then he immediately made a point to direct his gaze at both of them. "You'd be welcome too, of course, Mary. I just figured you'd be going home to Herb."

"You figured correctly," Mary said. "But I think Kaylee is free. I'd be happy to take Bear home with me. Herb loves having

Bear around. You could pick him up after dinner."

"I hate to put you out," Kaylee protested.

Mary shook her head. "It wouldn't put me out a bit. I'm sure Lily's up for a playdate with her favorite dog."

Reese shoved his hands into his jacket pockets. "I don't want to pressure you. You've had a stressful week, and I can understand if you want to go home and relax instead."

"No." A pang of guilt shot through Kaylee. She hadn't meant to give the impression she was rejecting Reese. "I'd be delighted to have dinner with you. It'll be fun."

"Great," Mary said brightly. "Now you two run along. I'll close up and get home with Bear. Go on."

Kaylee and Reese were practically shoved out the door, barely giving Kaylee time to grab her coat. But once they got to O'Brien's and settled at a quiet table, Kaylee had to admit it was good to have a nice, normal dinner with a friend.

"Thanks so much for inviting me," she said.

"I can't imagine anyone's company I'd enjoy more," he said, meeting her gaze with his sparkling blue eyes.

She felt her cheeks warm at the appreciation she saw there, and she cast around for a conversational topic that wouldn't rattle her so much. "Are you caught up with your handyman work since getting back?"

Reese chuckled. "I'm not sure I'm ever caught up."

A server seemed to appear almost out of nowhere, ready to take their order. Kaylee hadn't even opened the menu, but she'd been there often enough to make her decision without it. Reese hadn't bothered with his either since he was generally a steak-and-potatoes guy.

As soon as the server left, Reese said, "I ran into Nick today. I'm glad to hear the murder investigation is nearly over. Turtle Cove can go back to being cold and uneventful until spring."

"I'd welcome uneventful right now," Kaylee agreed, though she wasn't as sure as Nick that the investigation was close to finished. "There are still unanswered questions."

Reese held up a hand. "Let's not talk about unanswered questions or murder. What if I tell you about Mrs. Hanson's ghost instead?"

Kaylee raised her eyebrows. "Ghost?"

"Well, that's what she thought." He launched into a story of squirrels in the attic of Mrs. Hanson's cottage, and the efforts he'd had to go through to get them out and keep them out. "The funniest part was poor Mrs. Hanson. She was so disappointed that her cottage wasn't haunted. I think she was planning to start giving tours."

The image of the tiny, elderly Mrs. Hanson giving haunted house tours made Kaylee giggle. The server brought their food, and the rest of the meal was spent in light, friendly conversation. Once or twice, Kaylee noticed Reese watching her, and she felt an odd flutter in her stomach. She scolded herself for being silly. *You'd think I was already reading those romance novels Mary tried to talk me into.*

After supper, Reese drove her to the flower shop to get her car, but Kaylee put a hand on his arm when he started to get out. "You don't have to walk me to my car," she said. "It's bad enough you wouldn't let me pay for my share of dinner."

"Are you kidding? If my mom heard I invited a lady to dinner and let her pay, she'd box my ears," Reese said. "And the same for letting you walk to your car in the dark."

"Well, you'll have to protect your poor ears," Kaylee said as she turned up the collar on her coat. "Because I am going to walk to my car just fine. Thanks for supper. Stop fussing."

Reese held up both hands. "Okay. But in that case, you have to text me when you get home so I won't worry."

"I think that your request still qualifies as fussing, but I'll accept the compromise." She smiled at him, then hopped out of the truck and headed to where she'd parked her SUV. Though it was fully dark, the streetlights cast enough glow to keep her from running into anything. She'd reached her car and slipped the key in the lock when she heard footsteps behind her.

It's nothing. Just get in the car and stop being silly.

A heavy hand came down on her shoulder. She screamed.

18

"I'm so sorry," Bart stammered. "I was out for a walk. I saw you and wanted to say goodbye. I should have realized that would be startling. I truly am sorry."

Kaylee pressed her palm against her chest where it felt as if her heart might pound its way out. "It isn't your fault. I was caught up in my own thoughts and didn't hear you. It's all right."

"It's not really." He smiled ruefully. "I should have announced myself better."

Kaylee dropped her hand and managed a smile in return. "You're leaving Orcas Island?"

"No choice. My job can only be without me for so long. With Jeanette's killer caught, I need to go home." He sighed deeply. "I need to *be* home."

"I can understand that." Kaylee examined Bart closely. Even by the shadowy light from the nearby street lamp, she could tell he was completely worn out. "How much have you heard?"

He rubbed his hand over the beard stubble on his chin. "You mean did I hear Jeanette had embezzled? I heard."

"Was it news to you?"

He shoved his hands into the pockets of his coat and stared out into the night. "Yes. Jeanette was always a wild card. I could never guess what she might do at any given time. It's one of the things that made her exciting to be around." He shook his head. "She never even hinted at what she was up to. I wouldn't have gone along with it."

Kaylee tried to think of a gentle way to bring up Jeanette's plan to fake her own death. Finally she simply said, "It sounds as though she must have at least guessed that."

"Because she was going to fake her own death?" Bart huffed. "The deputy told me everything, though I think he did it mostly so he could gauge my reaction, try to figure out if I was surprised by anything he was saying. I've never been a suspect in anything before. I can't say I care for it."

"It's the sheriff's department's job to find the truth," Kaylee said diplomatically.

"You're right. Don't mind me. It's all been stressful." Again his gaze slipped to the darkness beyond them. "Jeanie said she thought we'd get back together. She said she loved me." He looked sharply at Kaylee. "Do you think that was a lie?"

"You'd be a better judge of her than I would."

He gave a dry, mirthless laugh. "I don't think I knew her any better than anyone else. I used to think the days after the divorce were the worst I'd ever face. I was so wrong." He blinked rapidly for a moment. "I suspect the house is going to feel even emptier when I get home."

His remark about the empty house gave her a thought. "Do you remember the cat from the inn? They want to find her a permanent home, and you seemed to like her. And cats don't mind being alone quite as much as dogs, so she'd be fine while her owner was at work. You two might find you help each other."

Bart watched her, his expression thoughtful. "She did seem nice."

"She's lovely," Kaylee said kindly. She actually thought Lucky was a bit of a feline Jekyll and Hyde, but having another creature depending on him might help the poor man through his grief.

"I'll ask them about it at the inn. Thanks." Bart shuffled off into the night.

Kaylee watched him until he disappeared completely in the darkness. Shaking off the gloom trying to settle on her, Kaylee turned to her car, but a loud crash from the narrow space between The Flower Patch and Death by Chocolate drew her attention.

"Jess?" she called. "Is that you?"

Kaylee walked toward the sound and saw one of the garbage cans on its side, rolling gently back and forth. She paused, wondering if an animal had knocked it over to rummage in its contents.

Her imagination conjured an image of Jessica lying in the darkness. *That's ridiculous. She went home hours ago.* But the mental picture wouldn't go away.

"Jessica?" Kaylee called louder. "Are you all right?" She walked to the very edge of the area that none of the lights touched, a pool of darkness and shadow. "Hello?"

Another crash made Kaylee leap back. She could barely make out a figure jumping up from behind the rest of the trash cans and sprinting away into the night.

"Hey!" Kaylee shouted. "What are you doing?"

But whoever it had been, was long gone.

Kaylee backed up until she was standing in the brightest pool of light the street lamps offered, then called Nick, noting that Jessica's car was gone, so she'd been right that her friend wasn't at the bakery.

When Nick answered, she described the situation quickly. "I don't see anyone now, so it's probably too late for you to do anything."

"You're still there?" Nick yelped. "What are you doing? Go get in your car right now. And stay on the phone while you do it so I can hear you got there safely."

Since Nick couldn't see her, Kaylee rolled her eyes at what felt like a massive overreaction, but she headed to her car and got in. "I'm all safe now."

"Good. I'll drive over and check out the area behind the shops, maybe cruise the surrounding streets. I'll call you if I see anything."

"Thanks. By the way, just before I heard the noise, I had a chat with Bart. He says he's leaving the island since the murder is solved."

"I hadn't heard that," Nick said. "But it's his right. How did he seem?"

"Sad, upset, exhausted," Kaylee said. "I think he truly loved her."

"Could be. You go on home. I'm at my car now."

When the call ended, Kaylee slipped the phone in her coat pocket and headed for Mary's house. She was a little annoyed that the relaxed mood she'd been in after her dinner with Reese had evaporated completely. She felt worried and wound up again.

Mary greeted her at the door with Bear dancing at her feet. Kaylee scooped him up and gave him a hug. "I missed you."

"Really?" Mary smirked. "You had dinner with the most attractive man on the island and you missed Bear?"

"Hey," Herb hollered from the next room. "Should I be worried about this?" He walked out to join his wife. "I had no idea you felt that way about Reese."

Mary bumped his shoulder playfully with hers. "Well, in case you wear out, I thought I'd keep an eye out for my second husband."

Herb laughed. "You might as well give up that idea. I'm sticking around for the long haul." He flung an arm around her and hugged her. The two were nearly the same height and looked very much like they belonged together.

"It's just as well," Mary said. "I think Reese only has eyes for Kaylee."

"Reese and I are good friends," Kaylee said, though she knew her statement lacked some of the conviction she'd once felt. Sure, she'd noticed some sparks between them lately, but she was probably making them up because of all the emotional upheaval on the island this week. She quickly forced her attention away from Reese before it brought on the inevitable blushing. "I ran into Bart after dinner with Reese. He's really devastated."

"Who's that?" Herb asked.

"The ex-husband of the dead woman." Mary cocked her head. "Don't you remember him from your mail route?"

A retired mail carrier, Herb had once known everyone on the island—or at least their names. "Oh yes," he said, "now I remember. Never met him, though."

"Did he say anything about Lyle?" Mary asked Kaylee.

"Not really," Kaylee answered. "But he'd heard about Jeanette's embezzling."

"Embezzling!" Herb exclaimed. "Sometimes it's like we're living in a cop show, one of the outlandish ones full of shocking twists."

Mary gave Herb a raised eyebrow, but didn't comment on his remark. Instead she asked, "Was Mr. Marlow aware Jeanette had been stealing from her work?"

"He said he didn't know, and I believed him." Kaylee shook her head sadly. "He seems to be a broken man."

Herb crossed his arms over his chest. "That still doesn't mean he didn't kill her. If I were to bump off Mary in a fit of rage, I'd be pretty torn up about it after."

"You've never had a fit of rage in your whole life," Mary said.

He scowled at her, though there was a twinkle in his eye. "I could be storing up."

"Well, I would offer to stay and protect you," Kaylee said, "but I think Bear and I are about ready to go home." She set him down to snap his leash to his collar.

"Oh, hold on. You forgot something at the shop." Mary hurried out of the room.

Kaylee tried to think of what she might have left behind, but nothing came to her. She smiled warmly at Herb. "Thanks for watching Bear for me."

"He's always welcome," Herb said. "I love dogs, even after being barked and growled at on my mail route every day for so many years. Now, I'll admit to preferring cats, but Bear is a gem among dogs."

"Speaking of cats, where's Lily?" Kaylee asked.

Herb laughed. "Oh, she played with Bear for a while, then went upstairs when she got tired of him. If I had to guess, I'd say she's napping on my pillow. She does that whenever she's miffed about something downstairs."

Kaylee grinned. "A wise cat."

Mary came into the entry and handed Kaylee the book she'd gotten from Between the Lines. "You left it at the shop. You'd said you planned to spend some time reading it, so I thought I'd bring it home."

"As I recall, you confiscated it and then shoved me out the door in your latest attempt at matchmaking, but thanks for giving it back. I do want to spend some time reading it. Though probably not tonight. I'm about done in."

"Do you want some coffee or tea to help you wake up before you make that drive?" Mary asked.

"No thank you. It's not that far, and I'm not that tired yet. Besides, if I drink caffeine now, I'll never sleep." She reached out and hugged Mary. "Thanks again for taking care of Bear. I'm sure he loved the visit."

"No more than we did," Mary said. "By the way, I flipped through the book a little. It mentions valerian root. I might get some for Lily."

"Really?" Kaylee said, making a mental note to read that entry. "Smith Hooper said he provides some to a holistic vet in Eastsound. Maybe he'd sell you some directly."

"Smith is a good guy," Herb said. "I should call him."

"Shame on us, holding Kaylee up when she just told us how ready she is to get home." Mary gave her another quick hug. "You go on now. And drive safely."

"I will," Kaylee promised. She held the book against her chest and ducked outside before they could come up with any new topics of discussion. To her dismay, she saw a light drizzle had begun, making the cold even more unpleasant as she and Bear dashed for the car.

As she climbed in, she suddenly wondered why Mary would want valerian root for her cat. Maybe Lily needed something calming during thunderstorms. The calico had been a rescue kitten and had probably experienced a few scary storms when she was tiny. *Mary's so sweet.*

Shivering slightly, she cranked up the heat and drove into the night, ready for the long day to be over.

19

On Sunday, Kaylee was more than ready for some quiet contemplation at Mustard Seed Community Church. The sermon's message was about making wise choices. "We hear so many voices," the pastor said. "But Scripture says the sheep know the voice of the Shepherd and will follow no other. So be kind. Be thoughtful. But also be wise. Not everyone speaks the truth."

"That's for sure," Kaylee muttered under her breath. She thought about all the things she'd heard about Jeanette and those around her. Which of those things were true? Even the evidence against Lyle might have been planted, though she couldn't imagine how.

After the service, Kaylee spotted Mary chatting with Jessica and DeeDee in the foyer. She hurried over to join them. "Impromptu Petal Pushers meeting?"

DeeDee chuckled. "Not quite, but I was saying we've postponed and canceled too many meetings lately. The weather has been atrocious, but I miss our talks."

"None of us are growing anything," Jessica said. "It's too early even to start things indoors. I think that's why we've let the weather scare us off for the last couple weeks."

"True," DeeDee said. "But we could hang out and eat and at least *pretend* to talk about gardening."

"I thought that's what we usually did," Kaylee joked.

Mary laughed. "I suspect you're missing Jess's amazing goodies, DeeDee."

"Well," DeeDee said. "That too."

Mary tapped Kaylee on the arm. "At least Kaylee has a new book she could tell us about. After she reads it anyway."

"I practically fell into bed when I got home last night so I haven't even opened it," Kaylee confessed. "I made it through feeding Bear and giving him a short walk and that was it."

"What book?" DeeDee asked, her professional interest clearly piqued.

"The one you ordered for her about toxic plants," Mary answered.

"Oh." DeeDee's face fell. "I thought we were talking about a novel."

"You're studying toxic plants?" Jessica asked.

"I thought it might be helpful for the consulting I do for the sheriff," Kaylee explained, then laughed. "But so far, Mary has read more of the book than I have."

"Only the one section on valerian," Mary said. "It mentioned that cats love valerian root as much as catnip. In fact, cats who aren't interested in catnip can often be enticed with valerian root."

"That's why you wanted some for Lily?" Kaylee was surprised. "I didn't think anything could be as attractive to cats as catnip."

"Oh, valerian is," Mary said. "Apparently they'll tear up the plant if you grow it outside because it's mostly the root that attracts them. And the book said that's interesting since valerian root is a sedative for people and dogs but a stimulant for cats. Isn't it amazing how differently something can affect different creatures?"

"Like chocolate," Jessica said. "Yummy for us, deadly for dogs."

"Exactly." Mary nudged Kaylee. "You're awfully quiet all of a sudden."

"I was thinking about Lucky, the cat from the inn," Kaylee said. "She was desperate to get into Margaret Olber's purse."

"I have trouble imagining Lucky being desperate for anything,"

DeeDee said with a laugh. "That is the most relaxed cat I've ever seen. Zoe drags her around like a rag doll."

"But she wasn't relaxed at all around Margaret," Kaylee insisted. "What if Margaret had a vial of valerian root in her purse?"

"That would be a little strange," Mary said doubtfully. "Quite a coincidence for Jeanette's brother and Margaret Olber to both be carrying around the plant that drugged Roz."

"Unless it's the same vial," Kaylee mused. "What if Margaret had it, and it ended up in Lyle's pocket in time for him to be arrested? He seemed to be as confused by its presence as anyone."

"I am inclined to believe you read too many mystery books." DeeDee frowned in thought. "How would she have gotten it to him? Had they met?"

"They might have, but I doubt it," Kaylee said.

"And he's not exactly someone who would let a strange woman come up and hug him so she could sneak something into his pocket," Mary said. "He isn't a particularly friendly person."

"That's true. Though I suppose she might have simply passed him in the hallway and dropped it in his coat pocket." Kaylee wondered if the same could have been true for the bit of scarf in his pocket. That would have been trickier. Still, the idea was worth considering, and she intended to talk to Nick about it.

Kaylee tuned back into her friends' conversation just as DeeDee was saying, "I can't believe someone left that poor kitty behind at the inn. She is a sweetie."

"Are you thinking about keeping her?" Mary asked. "Cats can grow on a person."

"No way," DeeDee said. "Though I'm beginning to suspect I need to find a home for her sooner rather than later. The girls don't seem to be too attached yet, but that could change pretty quickly."

"I suggested Bart Marlow take her," Kaylee said. "He seemed to enjoy her at the inn. And he was talking about how lonely his empty house would be."

"An excellent idea." DeeDee rubbed her hands together. "I'll see if I can make it happen."

Kaylee chatted with her friends for a few more minutes, all the while resisting the urge to call Nick about her latest theory.

She finally slipped away from the rest of the Petal Pushers and stepped outside, where she nearly walked right into Reese.

He gently caught her shoulders to avoid a collision. "Wow, you seem to be in your own world. Penny for your thoughts?"

The question made Kaylee laugh. "Aren't you a little young for that expression?"

Reese shrugged, grinning. "What can I say? I'm the fix-it guy for a lot of elderly people. The question still stands. What has you so distracted? Something tells me it isn't spiritual contemplation of the sermon today."

"It was a great sermon," Kaylee insisted. "But I was actually hunting for a quiet spot to call Nick."

Reese's grin vanished and concern filled his blue eyes. "What happened? Are you all right?"

"I'm fine. Mary mentioned something she read about valerian in one of my books. I ought to tell Nick about it."

Reese sighed in relief. "Good. How about I wait on you and we can go have brunch?"

"That's kind of you, but I hate to leave Bear home alone. Why don't you come over? I made a quiche and was going to warm it up. There's plenty." Then her voice grew teasing. "Unless you're one of those people who doesn't eat quiche."

"Egg pie? I love it. You make your call, and I'll follow you to your house."

Kaylee called Nick and shared what she'd learned. "Do you see?" she said finally. "It suggests that Margaret had the valerian root at some point."

"Or the cat was simply being wacky," Nick said. "I don't want to rain on your parade, Kaylee, but I don't know how far to trust the crazy behavior of a cat as evidence."

"So, you won't look into it?" she asked.

He issued a deep sigh. "Of course I will, if only to stop you from doing it yourself. I'll talk to the Olber woman. I wanted to chat with her about those coworkers of Jeanette's anyway. I don't think Bart is a serious suspect anymore, and I think it's just a matter of time before Lyle comes clean, but I don't want to be accused of not being thorough."

"Will you pass along whatever you find out?" Kaylee asked.

"Naturally," Nick said with faux melodrama. "Heaven forbid I not keep you in the loop on an open investigation."

When he disconnected the call, Kaylee stuck her tongue out at the phone.

Reese had been standing nearby, keeping enough distance to give her some privacy, but he chuckled as she made the face. "I take it Nick is in the doghouse?"

"He's okay," Kaylee said, not wanting to talk more about Nick's frustrating lack of seriousness about her tip. She linked her arm through Reese's. "Let's go have lunch."

He patted her hand. "Bring on the egg pie."

Over lunch, Kaylee made a point to ask Reese about his various handyman jobs. She sometimes worried that she spent too much time focused on her investigations and not enough time paying attention to her friends. Besides, Reese's descriptions of various jobs he'd done could be very funny.

Kaylee was giggling over a story about the time he found a

squirrel leafing through old hymnals in the storage room of the church when the phone rang. She hopped up to dig it out from the pocket of her coat as Reese was saying, "It took me a long time to find out where he'd gotten in, but probably not as long as it took him to learn that hymn."

Laughing, Kaylee crossed the room and Bear roused himself enough to move from his spot near the heating grate. He followed her in case she might be heading outside for a walk. "Sorry, Bear," Kaylee said as she held up the phone. "Just a phone call."

With a sigh, Bear flopped down at her feet. Kaylee checked the display and saw it was Nick calling. *I guess he meant it about updating me after all.* "Hi, Nick. What did Margaret Olber say?"

"Nothing," he said. "Not to me anyway. She wasn't in her room, and the folks at the inn say she hasn't been there since yesterday."

"Are they sure?" Kaylee asked, the hairs rising on the back of her neck.

"If she came back, she snuck by them. And she apparently insisted that no one enter her room during her stay, not even cleaning staff. So no one has been inside."

"That's not suspicious at all," Kaylee said sarcastically.

"Not suspicious enough. She's not a suspect, so I can't get a warrant to see the inside of her room, not that warrants are the easiest thing to get on Sunday anyway. We'll keep an eye out for her, and I'll talk to her when she shows up, but that's about all I can do."

"But Nick—"

"No buts, Kaylee," Nick said firmly, and Kaylee recognized his deputy voice, which he rarely used on her. "I can't do anything else right now. It's Sunday. I'm asking you to forget about this case for the rest of the day. Read one of your plant books. Walk your dog. Maybe spend time with someone."

"Did you have anyone in mind, since you're being bossy?"

"Reese wouldn't be a bad choice. This will keep until tomorrow. Go do something for yourself for once."

Kaylee felt herself blushing, particularly since she was already spending time with Reese. "Nick, a woman was killed. How am I supposed to let it go?"

"You're a smart girl. You'll manage. Goodbye," he said, and the line went dead in her ear.

"If Nick knew how unhappy you appear after every conversation with him today, it would be a terrible blow to his ego," Reese observed with a grin.

"I think Nick's ego can handle it," Kaylee said with more vinegar in her tone than she'd intended. "He couldn't find Margaret Olber. Apparently she's missing."

"Missing?"

"The inn says she hasn't returned," Kaylee said. "And Nick can't get into her room to search for clues. Apparently she left instructions that no one was to enter her room during her stay, including cleaning staff. So without a warrant, they're not letting Nick in. All he can do is have the department keep an eye out for her."

"And you don't think that's enough," Reese said.

"I think it's suspicious. She had valerian root in her purse—I'm sure of it. What if she didn't know it was there? What if someone planted it on several possible suspects and simply waited for the sheriff to pick one? And what if that person is cleaning up loose ends now?"

"Do you think that's a bit far-fetched?"

Kaylee folded her arms and frowned. "You sound like Nick."

Reese held up his hands. "He's not necessarily wrong."

"Well, it was great sharing egg pie with you," Kaylee said tartly, fueled by growing exasperation, "but Bear and I are going over to the hotel. I'll clean up these brunch dishes when I get home."

"In that case," Reese said. "I'm going with you. We can take your vehicle or mine. Your choice." His voice was amiable enough, but she caught a glint of iron in his eyes.

Kaylee considered balking since she didn't enjoy being told what to do, but she was tempted by the idea of having someone along with her. She finally said, "My car will be fine."

Reese reached for his coat. "Ready when you are."

At the inn, Kaylee found Stella Dunmore at the front desk once more. As soon as she saw Kaylee, Bear, and Reese heading her way, she said, "If this is about Margaret Olber, she still hasn't returned."

"What makes you think it's about her?" Kaylee asked.

Stella shrugged. "I guessed. And I kind of heard Deputy Durham muttering your name when he was here searching for her."

Behind her, Kaylee heard Reese give a cough that sounded as if it had initially been a chuckle.

"I'm concerned about Margaret," Kaylee said.

Stella eyed her suspiciously. "Yes ma'am."

"Are you totally sure that Margaret isn't in her room?" Kaylee asked.

"No one saw her come in, and no one has heard a peep from that room," Stella said.

"However, it's not as if there is only one door to this inn," Kaylee said. "And you're lightly staffed this time of year. What if she came in while you were doing something else, something that drew you away from the front desk?"

Stella shifted nervously. "That does happen sometimes. But she hasn't made any noise at all, and she watched a lot of television when she was in the room. In fact, one of the other guests complained about her leaving it on all night."

"But no one has been in there," Kaylee insisted.

"Because she said she didn't want anyone in her room."

"Yes, but what if she's in there, and so ill that she can't even call out?" Kaylee asked. "She could be hoping someone will come in and find her."

Stella pressed her lips together. "We have no reason to think that's true."

"Fine," Kaylee said. "At least walk up with me while I knock on the door. Maybe we'll hear something inside."

Stella seemed torn, and Kaylee waited while the desk clerk thought it over. She noticed Reese giving her a reproving frown. He probably didn't appreciate the spot she was putting the young woman in, but she felt more and more sure that they needed to get into Margaret's room.

"Fine," Stella said. "We'll go up, and you can knock. I'm not promising anything, though. Unless she calls out for help, I won't unlock the door."

Since Kaylee knew she wasn't going to get a better response than that, she headed for the stairs, with Bear at her side and Stella and Reese right behind her. When they reached Margaret's room, Kaylee pounded on the door. "Margaret, are you in there? It's me, Kaylee." She pressed her ear to the door, hoping for any sound from inside.

"Do you hear anything?" Stella asked.

Kaylee glanced at the young woman and, for the briefest instant, she considered saying that she had, but she couldn't bring herself to lie. Instead, her shoulders slumped. "No I didn't. But the door is thick. She could be in there."

"Maybe I could try?" Reese offered. "My voice might carry better."

Kaylee stepped out of the way, and Reese took hold of the doorknob and called through the door. "Margaret? Are you in there?"

Reese turned the knob. To their shock, the door swung open. With a yap, Bear raced through the cracked door, pulling his leash right out of Kaylee's hand.

"Bear!" she called. "Get back here." She turned to Stella. "I don't need you to let me in after all."

Stella stood shaking her head. "You shouldn't go in there."

"I've got to get my dog," Kaylee said.

"Who knows what Bear might do in there?" Reese added.

Stella waved her hands. "Fine. Get the dog. Just please don't touch anything."

Kaylee pushed the door the rest of the way open. "Bear, come."

Once the door was fully open, they could see Bear sitting in the middle of Margaret Olber's open suitcase in the center of the room, his jaw clamped around a shoe. All around him, the room looked as if it had endured a hurricane. Clothes were strewn everywhere. Drawers hung open. Toiletries were scattered across the bathroom. The bed was in utter disarray.

Kaylee surveyed the mess, openmouthed. What had happened here? Had someone searched Margaret's room when she wasn't there? Or worse yet, had someone attacked Margaret in her room?

"I think we need to call Nick," Reese said.

Kaylee and Stella bobbed their heads in unison. Whatever had happened in that hotel room, it was time to get the authorities involved.

20

By the time Kaylee got home, the afternoon had slipped into evening. She was worn out, and Reese apparently was too. After walking her to the door, he bid her a brief good night and drove off.

Kaylee walked Bear around the cottage, but he seemed less interested than usual in sniffing every shrub along the way. When they got inside, he happily flopped on the small dog cushion in the kitchen and napped while Kaylee had a soothing cup of tea.

She sat sipping the hot beverage and thinking about Margaret. Now two women had vanished in the area, and Kaylee hoped desperately that Margaret's story turned out differently than Jeanette's.

She felt the rumble of her phone in her jacket pocket. *Please be Nick with good news.* She fished out the phone and saw a number she didn't recognize. As soon as she answered the call, a terrified whisper came over the line. "Your boat! They're on your boat!"

"They who?" Kaylee asked. "Who is this? Have you called the police?"

"Oh no," the caller whispered. "They see me." The call ended.

Kaylee stared at the phone. The voice had been so soft and whispery that she couldn't even be sure if it was a man or a woman. *A woman, I think.*

Why would anyone be on her boat? She kept the *KayBea* moored at a small marina in West Sound and she hadn't visited it for weeks. During the winter, her visits to the boat were few and far between, and then it was only to check on it. She wasn't interested in being out in winter waves and weather.

With a frown, she called Nick.

His phone went to voice mail. "Nick," Kaylee said. "Someone called about trespassers on my boat. Will you go check on it? You know where it's moored."

Hanging up, Kaylee chewed on her lower lip. Should she let it go and wait to hear from Nick? She called Reese, but got his voice mail too. She left a message similar to the one she'd left for Nick.

"I'll wait," she said, getting a sleepy look from Bear. "I don't have to go out there. That wouldn't be wise."

Bear must have agreed because he lowered his head to his paws. Kaylee sat down and sipped her tea, which was getting cold. *Going out there would be foolish. It's exactly the kind of stupid thing television characters do all the time, and it always ends badly.* She took another determined sip of tea, ignoring its unappealing temperature.

Finally, she set the cup on the table and gave up. There was no way she was going to be able to simply ignore the call and wait for Nick. *If I leave now, I'll probably arrive when he and Reese do. They can scold me for being there.* She stood again, this time not even getting a glance from the sleeping dog. "I won't make you go with me," she said softly.

Kaylee's little boat, the *KayBea*, had once belonged to her grandfather, who had named it for Kaylee and her grandmother, Bea. It was a connection to the grandfather she loved, so she hoped desperately that no one was stealing or vandalizing it. As she drove to West Sound, she prayed softly under her breath that her grandpa's boat was undamaged.

She made the drive to the nearby town a little more quickly than was strictly wise on the dark roads, but they were empty of traffic so she made it to the West Sound marina without incident.

Once there, she found the boat quiet. Even by the soft light of the moon, she could see no one was on deck. "A prank call," Kaylee muttered as she climbed aboard. "That's a great way to end the day."

It wasn't until she was in the boat that she noticed the large duffel that shouldn't have been there. She wouldn't have left a duffel on the boat, and certainly not on deck where the weather could get to it. *Someone was here.*

"About time you got here."

The voice was familiar, though Kaylee had never heard it used with such vitriol. She spun to see Margaret smiling coldly at her from the dock, though Kaylee gave her expression barely a glance. The gun in the woman's hand was too distracting.

"What are you doing out here?" Kaylee asked, her entire body tense with sudden fear.

"I need a ride to the mainland, and you're going to give it to me. If you're very good, you might even survive the trip." Margaret's gaze stayed tightly focused on Kaylee, even as she untied the boat's line and tossed it onto the deck.

Something in the woman's tone made Kaylee doubt very much that she would survive the trip if she allowed her boat to leave the marina. Kaylee waved toward the duffel. "Was that Jeanette's? She told Roz it held a raft."

"Roz is a moron, plain and simple," the woman growled as she stepped onto the boat. Kaylee watched her closely but the gun never wavered. "That bag holds the money Jeanette stole from the company. Well, most of it."

"What happened to the rest of it?" Kaylee asked, backing away from her.

"Some she spent in preparation for her escape, I suppose," Margaret said. "And some she gave to me. You see, I discovered her theft. She thought she was so clever. Imagine her shock when I went to her apartment and confronted her before she left. That's when she offered me a bribe to postpone my discovery until after her disappearance."

"So you knew she intended to fake her own death." Kaylee allowed her gaze to drift to the side of the boat. If she jumped overboard, she could probably get under the pier where Margaret couldn't shoot her... but how long would she last in the icy water?

Margaret was clearly enjoying telling her story. "She told me all about it. She was very proud of her plan. She even got my bribe money out of that duffel *right in front of me*. From then on, all I could think about was how my life could be better if I took it away from her."

"Why did she have so much money in cash?"

Margaret shrugged. "She didn't say. It wasn't near the top of my list of questions. I was mostly focused on how I could take it for myself."

"Why didn't you attack her then and there?" Kaylee asked. "Why let her come here at all?"

"I couldn't be sure that no one had seen me enter her apartment that night. Besides, she had a plan to disappear here. It seemed a much smarter choice to make use of that."

"So you took her off Roz's boat."

"I did. I followed them in a boat I 'borrowed.'" Margaret smiled tightly. "And when I showed up, Jeanette still didn't have sense enough to be worried. I told her that Pop had chickened out on her because of the weather. She was grateful for my help, right up to the end. Can you believe that?"

"She trusted you, and you killed her," Kaylee said, letting her disgust ooze into her voice. "And then you framed her brother."

"But he was such an easy target. And surprisingly open to someone who agreed with him about that Corzo woman. After listening to him rant and snivel, I planted enough evidence on him to keep the investigation pointed right where I wanted it."

"So that's why you came to the island even after Jeanette disappeared? To find yourself a patsy?"

Margaret laughed cruelly. "Between that and all my shopping, I've had a very enjoyable vacation."

"And you don't mind seeing someone else pay for what you did?"

"Hardly." Margaret's eyes narrowed. "Enough stalling. It's time we got going. I checked and we have plenty of fuel for the trip. I've made quite a study of you, Kaylee Bleu. I guessed you'd be the sort to take good care of her boat."

"How did you even find out I had a boat?" Kaylee asked.

"Are you kidding? The people of Turtle Cove *love* to gossip, especially about pretty, single women. Though I did expect to find it on your property." She yawned theatrically. "You won't believe how many boring conversations I had to have to find out you keep it here."

"On my property?" Kaylee echoed. "So it was you outside my house."

Margaret shook the gun at Kaylee. "I said enough stalling. Don't make me tell you again. We need to get going."

"Where?" *Reese, Nick, where are you?*

"I'll tell you on the way. Now start up the engine or I'll go ahead and kill you now and drive the boat myself. I can roll your dead body overboard once we're far enough out on the water. I've had practice."

"So much for how I might survive this."

Margaret laughed coldly, and Kaylee winced.

Realizing she didn't have any other options, Kaylee walked to the boat's controls. Margaret moved very little, not getting any closer. *I guess she doesn't want to risk my doing something desperate.*

Kaylee turned the engine over and it cranked smoothly. *For once, I wish Reese didn't keep the boat in such good repair for me.*

She'd barely pulled away from the marina when a bright light shone directly on Margaret. It was nearly blinding from Kaylee's angle so she couldn't imagine what it must be like for the other woman.

A voice issued from a bullhorn. "Stop right there!" Kaylee would recognize that gruff bellow anywhere. It was Roz. "I have the sheriff's department on board. Halt and prepare to be boarded."

Margaret raised the gun, clearly intending to shoot blindly toward the spotlight.

Without stopping to think, Kaylee grabbed the duffel and swung it, striking Margaret in the back. The pistol fired, but it was already pointing toward the water.

Stumbling with the gun still in her hand, Margaret tried to catch herself. Kaylee swung again, hitting Margaret in the side this time. The taller woman tripped, slamming into the railing and going over into the black water surrounding the boat.

"Man overboard!" Kaylee yelled.

"Don't worry," Nick called back. "We'll get her. And if that's evidence you're slinging around, would you please set it down before it goes overboard too?"

"Always complaining," Kaylee muttered as she dropped the heavy duffel on the deck. Her shoulders slumped in relief, and she took her first relaxed breath since she'd come aboard.

On Monday morning, Kaylee groaned when Reese walked into The Flower Patch. She held up her hand. "If you've come by to yell at me for not waiting for you or Nick before going out to the boat, he already beat you to it."

Reese shook his head. "I'm not here to scold, nag, or yell. I just wanted to make sure you're all right."

"Considering I didn't get much sleep last night, I'm actually doing great," Kaylee said. "I finally learned what happened to Jeanette. Her family and her friends can start to heal. Nick said Lyle and Bart both left on the morning ferry."

"I'm not sure how quickly anyone is going to heal," Reese said. "They're going to hear a lot of unpleasant things about Jeanette. Roz must be devastated."

"The truth isn't always kind," Kaylee agreed. "But judging from her face last night after they fished Margaret out of the water, she'll recover just fine."

Reese looked around. "Where's Bear?"

"Mary volunteered to take him for a walk. She's on Team Nick at the moment. She thinks I should have waited for you guys before going out to the boat, or at least taken Bear."

Reese grinned at that. "In this case, I suspect not having Bear gave you one less thing to worry about, so I'm okay with that. And everyone who is scolding you is doing it from love."

"So why are you *not* scolding me?" Kaylee teased. "I'm hurt."

"Don't be. I worry about you plenty," he said, his face serious. He issued a resigned sigh. "But I've figured out that none of us are ever going to change Kaylee Bleu." Then his serious expression softened. "And I realize that I wouldn't want you any other way."

Something in Reese's expression sent a warm flush to Kaylee's cheeks, and, for once, she admitted to herself that she enjoyed it. *I could get used to this feeling*, she thought with a smile. *Yes, I certainly could.*